CW00665888

Shameful
Addictions

Viktor Redreich

Redreich Publishing Limited

Free Book

Get your free book now

https://redreich.com/dirtysecrets

Published by Redreich Publishing Limited

71-75 Shelton Street, Covent Garden London WC2H 9JQ United Kingdom

Contents

Chapter One

Teeny bunny rabbit

Two teenaged girls skipped onto the stage, their identical dresses illuminated by strobes of pink and red light. The girls could have been twins, with their long pale blonde hair and delicate bodies. Meeting in the middle of the stage, the two kissed and held onto each other. One lifted her leg and hooked it around the other girl's waist, showing a flash of white panties with little pink hearts on them.

Charlotte put her hand to her own heart, feeling it flutter. The men in the audience shifted and murmured, clearly enjoying the sight of the two young women holding hands and pressing their plumped pink lips over each other's faces. Their excitement wasn't one she could join in on, or even understand. She felt like a woman watching a train wreck while all around her sadistic rubberneckers clapped and cheered for the disaster.

It was awful, absolutely terrible.

The girls held hands, facing a man who sat in the closest seat to the stage. They both smiled at him, for him, like they shared a secret. Turning together, still holding hands, the two girls skipped in a circle while their frilly dresses flounced around their forms. More was concealed than was shown, but it didn't feel like that at all. Charlotte was seeing so much more than she wanted to.

The girls came together and hugged, pushing their bouncy boobies against each others'.

From behind them, another girl mounted the stage, wearing fluffy pink cat ears and a cat tail. She posed, facing the audience, hooking her hands beside her face to form paws. Whiskers had been painted on her cheeks using makeup, and the tip of her nose was pink. The cat-girl turned and posed in the other direction.

Oh, goodness, no.

Charlotte had thought the tail was some sort of belt. The end of it went right through a hole in the cat-girl's skirt and panties. It was a butt plug.

"Damn," a man muttered. "Yeah."

Suddenly, confetti rained down upon the girls on the stage, reflective silver strips of paper that caught and shattered the pulsating light. The cat-girl jumped and pranced, pawing at the pieces of paper, while the identical teens kicked and danced through the fallen confetti like kids in a rain puddle.

Another shower of paper came after the first. Money, this time. The men in the audience were standing, throwing dollar bills onto the stage with abandon. Even in the low light, Charlotte saw the distinctive blue stripe of a $100. Ridiculous money. Ridiculous men.

A fourth girl pranced onto the scene, her dress composed almost entirely of frills and bows. She dove into the growing patch of money and tossed bills up into the air. The other three skipped around, flashing their panties while jumping up to catch the money, and bending over to pick it up off the ground.

Charlotte covered her eyes, unable to bear looking any longer at the spectacle in front of her. It was an absolute disgrace, what she was seeing, and she had no idea how anyone could tolerate it. Those girls were up there acting all cutesy and innocent while the men in the audience ogled their bodies, had sex with them with their eyes. Some were almost certainly taking pictures so they could repeatedly degrade those girls for as long and as often as they liked.

This is too much.

She shouldn't be there. A respectable career woman like herself shouldn't be in such a filthy, sexual place.

Unfortunately, she had no choice in the matter.

Charlotte stood up from her chair and left the stage area; out of the corner of her eye, she saw the cat-girl and the ribbon girl grinding their bodies together while the twins hiked up their skirts and flashed their panties again. She'd gotten out of there just in time, it seemed. The routine was getting too intense.

She staggered past the exit, the blessedly-dark exit. It took all of her self-control not to make a break for it. She kept going, working her way past a wall covered in photograph-worthy wall art. Unicorns and rabbits pranced around on the pink walls, beneath swooping rainbows and smiling suns. The name of the lounge, Club Lollipop, appeared in neon letters every few feet or so, as if she needed any reminding of where she was.

Charlotte found a table at the back of the lounge. The chair was a ridiculous thing, with pink fluff trimming on the edge of the seat cushion and the back. She grimaced as she sat down and put her head in her hands. An image of a bunny rabbit smiled up at her to reassure her everything would be okay.

None of this was okay.

Why on earth had Damian asked her to come cover this?

Charlotte had no idea how long she sat alone at that table, the bunny pulsing and flashing in front of her eyes. The cheerful music pumping in through the speakers dropped to a more acceptable level. Applause and cheers rang up to replace the music.

Seems like the routine is over, Charlotte thought.

A series of rapid clicking sounds came at her from the side. "Hi!" piped a chipper voice, in a very high and false manner. "I wanted to make sure you're enjoying yourself."

Charlotte lifted her head from her hands and looked over at the girl standing beside her. She almost fainted from shock. It was the cat-eared girl, the girl who had pranced around on the stage with a butt plug stuck between her pert ass cheeks for everyone to see. She had very big, bright blue eyes and silver-blonde hair. An ungodly amount of makeup caked her face. Charlotte could see where the cat-girl had reshaped her cheekbones and nose and chin, carving out new bone structure for herself using bronzer and highlighter. No doubt it was all meant to make her look much younger than she was, not that she was very old to begin with. If she was twenty, Charlotte would have been astonished.

The cat-girl made a funny meowing sound and tilted her head to the side. She brought her hands up under her chin, fingers curled to make them look like paws. "I really hope you're enjoying yourself. That's what this is all about!"

"Is it?" Charlotte asked, still feeling a bit faint. She thought she'd be observing from afar but now she was talking to one of the main "stars." That was, for her, the emotional equivalent of a meteorologist getting caught in a tornado.

"Yeah!" the girl squeaked in her high voice. "How can you not have fun? Meow! Maybe I can get you a drink."

Charlotte held up her hands. The shadowy silhouette of a man standing in the corner, a bouncer, shifted into view. Lollipop had a strict no-touching policy. Charlotte quickly put her hands down. "I'm, uh, fine. Thank you, young lady."

The girl laughed and bounced on her heels–her stiletto heels. "Lady? I'm a kitty! Well, okay. But if you need anything, just ask for the kitty."

Charlotte was saved from having to say anything else by the cat-girl scampering off to talk to another customer.

She was fairly certain she was in Hell. And this week had started off so normally. Her boss, Damian, sent her the usual list of videos she was to make. Charlotte was a video blogger under the payroll of a much larger company. Her video channel was very popular among teen girls, a demographic which was difficult for companies to target.

Damian told her what topics to cover in her videos, and it was up to Charlotte to figure out how best to present the material so the girls would pay attention, and bring in ad revenue. Typically, the videos were about things like skincare tips, and how to get over a crush, how to pursue a job and education at the same time, and other topics that were both trendy and open-minded.

Charlotte adored her work. Even thinking about it now was like a balm to her soul, calming her.

And then, she had noticed a strange video idea in the middle of the list. "Subverting Expectations: Why Sex Work is Real Work."

Charlotte looked around and noticed a waitress nearby. She lifted her hand to get the girl's attention. The waitress hopped over in an instant, literally hopping because of the bunny ear headband on her head and the cottontail plug shoved in her ass.

"What can I help you with?" the bunny-girl asked, using the same cutesy and high-pitched tone of voice as the other girl.

Charlotte licked her dry lips. The girl giggled. Charlotte covered her mouth, horrified at what that must have looked like. "Could I get some water, please? With lemon?"

The waitress widened her eyes. "You want some water, huh?"

"Yes, please. I'm a bit thirsty."

The waitress giggled and also covered her mouth. "Oh, I understand. *Water* it is. A lot or a little?"

"Just a glass."

"I'll get that for you." The waitress stuck out her ass and wiggled it at Charlotte, her puffy bunny tail bobbing up and down between her fleshy cheeks. Charlotte couldn't take her eyes off the puff. She imagined it had to be so uncomfortable having a wedge of plastic pushed up inside there like that. And then she forced herself to stop imagining it. The way things seemed to be going, she might have to find out for herself.

Damian had just smiled sheepishly at Charlotte when she confronted him in his office, demanding an explanation. Up until that point, she'd hoped it was a mistake, a typo, a funny autocorrect error they could both laugh about. But when Damian gave her that smirky, embarrassed smile, she knew she was wrong, and the floor had collapsed out from underneath her feet, leaving her with nothing to stand on.

"We've got new ownership," Damian had told her. "It doesn't take effect until Wednesday, so you can keep making your usual videos until then, but after that it has to be all new stuff."

"All?" Charlotte asked.

"Didn't you look at the rest of the list?"

She hadn't, at the time. She'd stopped when she got to that odd one. At Damian's urging, she had looked at the rest of the list.

"Different Styles of Sex Work"

"How to be a Real Woman"

"Virginity is a Social Construct."

Damian had spoken while she was still reeling, voice fading in and out of focus. "The fact of the matter is that our new owner isn't exactly in with the traditionalism and wholesomeness you promote. Family values and sex-negativity are out."

"I can't just switch my content over like that!" she had protested.

"Well, see, right before, you'll be doing a video on career choices. We're going to expect you to use that to segue into the one on sex work." Damian made it all sound so simple, so easy, as if this didn't go against everything she had built. "Your style of making videos and your accessibility is amazing. The owner wants to keep you and your channel, but you need to be more sex-positive from now on."

She had tried to protest again. "I don't know anything about sex work!"

But Damian had had an answer for that, too. "You will have to learn. Go to this club called Club Lollipop on Rim Street."

She had come, hoping it wouldn't be so bad.

But it was so much worse.

This video was meant to be all about how sex empowered the women who worked with it, but there wasn't anything empowering she could see in this place. Club Lollipop had turned sex, which she thought should be serious and valuable, into a cheap toy. These girls, in their dresses and cute outfits, were nothing more than dolls for men to play with.

"Here's your water!" the bunny-girl announced, startling Charlotte. She almost fell off her chair. A glass of clear liquid was set in front of her, wet moisture gleaming on the outside of the frosty glass. "I put it on your tab. I'm sure you'll be wanting more."

"I wanted lemon?"

The bunny-girl opened her eyes very wide. "We don't use real lemon. The peels are so-o-o *dirty*. I *squirted* a little something special in there for you, though."

"What?"

"Just kidding! It's only lemon juice!" The girl giggled and hopped off.

Charlotte picked up the glass and took a sip. The flavorless liquid struck her tongue, encapsulated her senses. It wasn't water. It was vodka. Straight vodka, with a touch of lemon. Choking, sinuses burning, Charlotte shoved the glass away, leaving a smear of condensation on the table. Tears stung her eyes from the powerful alcohol, from humiliation and guilt. Drinking was another serious subject on which she'd made videos. Charlotte had a few glasses of wine a year, mostly during holidays. To be handed a glass of vodka so casually by a hardly of age waitress was unfathomable, unthinkable. She'd never have imagined such a moment could ever exist.

I need to get out of here.

The music started up again, signaling that another stage routine was about to begin. Lights pulsed and danced, spinning in and out of each other, dizzying.

I need to stay, she told herself, arguing with her own sensibilities. She could have been laid off when the new owner bought the company. They had been very generous in keeping her on, rather than replacing her.

She owed them, that anonymous figure. Shouldn't she at least attempt to do a good job here?

The glass of vodka was much more appealing, suddenly. Charlotte picked it up and took another sip, letting the warmth scorch all the way through her. Already, her mind was buzzing, loosening from the effects of the alcohol.

Feeling a little braver, Charlotte stood up and took her drink over to the stage to get a better look at things.

Chapter Two

Petals in bloom

WITH ANOTHER DANCE ROUTINE behind her and half the glass of vodka in her system, Charlotte was ready to enter the second phase of her investigation. She'd observed and had seen far more than she'd ever planned to. Now it was time for her to get some answers to her burning questions, and damn, did she have a ton of them.

Charlotte stood up from her spot by the now-empty stage and cast an eye around the club. The pulsating lights didn't fool her for an instant. She saw the waitress from before right away, gyrating her hips in a male customer's face. His face was a rictus of pleasure as he writhed beneath her, gripping the sides of his chair. Every inch of his posture spoke of an intense desire to grab the girl and screw her.

I think I'm buzzed. Maybe a little more. Maybe I'm drunk.

Charlotte stared at the rabbit-tailed waitress until she finally hopped away from the man, who hurried off to the bathroom with one hand shoved into his pocket. And she kept staring until the waitress finally noticed her and scurried on over.

"Are you enjoying your drink?" the waitress asked, bobbing her head so her ears flopped and bounced. Her bosom, small, perky, mimicked the movement in a more restrained manner.

"Best water I've ever had." Charlotte took a sip from her glass. She'd long since stopped tasting the vodka and only felt it as a burn down her throat, under her chest, in her core. The only taste was that of lemon juice, like a pungent jab to the mouth.

The bunny-girl giggled. "Great. Can I get you anything else? A show, maybe?" She turned and bent over, sticking out her ass. Her cheeks were so firm that when she flexed them, they parted, showing a bit of the body of the buttplug underneath the cottony pouffe attached to the end.

A wave of acidic disgust roiled in Charlotte's stomach and made it almost all the way up to her mouth before she managed to fight it back down. She suddenly didn't feel as drunk. What she had just seen was going to haunt her for days, having burned itself into the retinas of her eyes.

Charlotte closed her eyes, saw the afterimage of the girl's rear on the backs of her eyelids. The pulsing lights of the club still made their way beneath the thin stretches of skin, blinking on and off, on and off.

"Hey, you don't look so good, miss. Maybe you need some actual water?"

Charlotte forced a smile to her lips and opened her eyes. "Actually, I'm fine. Thank you. A bit dizzy is all. I wanted to ask you something."

"Sure!" The girl brightened in an instant.

"How old are you?"

The change in mood occurred again just as fast as before. The waitress pursed her lips together. "I'm 18. Not that it's any of your business."

Charlotte mentally scolded herself for being so uncouth. She wasn't going to get any information that way. "I'm sorry. That came out wrong. I wanted to know more about the kind of girl who would work at a place like this. That sounds bad, too. I'm sorry. I'm usually better at this."

The waitress tilted her head, her bunny ears flopping over. For a moment, Charlotte feared she was about to be tossed out for prying in matters that didn't concern her. Then, the girl smiled wide and leaned in very close to Charlotte, whispering into her ear. "That's okay. I have that effect on a lot of people."

Her breath was uncomfortably warm.

Charlotte leaned away. The girl leaned with her. The slightest wrong move from either of them and they'd collapse together.

She thinks I'm flirting with her.

That definitely wasn't what she wanted. Or was it? Pretending that she was bad at flirting was an easier way to get information than to give up her whole life story. It wouldn't be good journalism, but Charlotte didn't think that mattered at this point. And the girl didn't have to tell her anything.

"What's your name?" Charlotte asked, backtracking.

"Robun."

"Robin?"

"Robun," Robun said, emphasizing the bun.

Charlotte finally got it. She supposed it was a mistake to expect an actual name. "Okay, Robun. What brings a girl like you to a place like this?"

Robun tapped her chin with her finger, playing up that she was thinking on it. Charlotte could tell she wasn't. Her gaze was clear and strong, not cloudy with remembrance at all. "Well, honestly, it doesn't matter what kind of girl I am! I was going to come here anyway."

"Wait, what do you mean by that?"

Robun smiled. "I just was! I had a job offer waiting. The owner paid for some of my cheerleading practices. He sponsored me. He does that with a lot of the girls, pretty much everyone here."

Charlotte couldn't believe her ears. What she was hearing couldn't be legal. "The owner of Lollipop?"

"Right! He picks out talent when he sees it and he, like, cultivates it, or something. I forget what words he uses." Robun beamed, as if being prepared for a life of what Charlotte viewed as sexual deviancy was something to be proud of. "He saw me and he liked me, so he made sure I could get better and better at the things I'm good at. And the pay here is great!"

"I see," Charlotte said faintly. She felt like she might pass out. "And he does that with the other dancers, too?"

Robun smiled, looking so young and beautiful, so easy to take advantage of. "Almost everyone here. Except for the bartender and the bouncer."

Charlotte licked her dry lips and set her vodka down on a nearby table. She'd had enough of it. "Can I talk to some of the other dancers?"

"You like to keep your options open, huh?" Robun wiggled her rear and her chest, shimmying. "You can talk to anyone you want. Just don't forget about me."

"I don't think I could if I tried." Charlotte rubbed her hand through her hair, very conscious of the way doing that made her clothes pull tight over her breasts. "The cat-girl."

"Oh, Katerina!"

Another terrible pun. She must be going insane. This couldn't be happening. "Yes. Katerina. Can I talk to her?"

The answer was, naturally, yes. Clubs like this existed to please their customers. Charlotte could have anything she wanted if she was willing to pay the price. As Katerina sauntered up to her, Charlotte wondered if she was willing to make that payment. Even if not doing this meant she lost her job, it might almost be worth it to get out of this.

"Hi, again!" Katerina mewed, coming up to Charlotte and arching her back, catlike. She wagged her ass, making her fluffy tail swish back and forth. "You asked for me?"

Charlotte grabbed hard at her inner strength and pulled it to the surface. Somehow, through sheer determination and force of will, she rearranged her lips into the shape of a passable smile. "I did. I'm curious about you, Kat. Can I call you Kat?"

Kat nodded. She draped the upper half of her body over Charlotte's table. Her boobs pushed flat against the smooth surface. "You can call me anything. I might not answer, though."

Charlotte kept her smile, though it was beginning to pain her. "Robun told me the club owner found her and gave her a job offer. Did the same thing happen to you?"

Kat smiled. "That's right! I took gymnastics in high school. I went through a growth spurt before my Sophomore year and couldn't afford a new uniform. Then Mamba stepped in."

"Mamba. Like the snake?"

"I guess so."

Wasn't that the perfect analogy? The snake, luring the helpless rabbit and kitten and all the other little creatures down a bad path.

"What did he do?"

"He said he'd been watching me and would pay for my uniform." Kat's smile grew smaller, a little more natural. "At first, I was scared of him. He's intimidating at first. But he said he saw talent in me and wanted me to be able to keep going. He even picked out the moves for the routine that won me the finals Senior year. He cultivated my talent."

There was that phrase again, said in almost exactly the same way. Charlotte's heart pounded against her ribs. "And when you graduated, he invited you to work here."

"He told me to come work for him long before I graduated." Kat shrugged one slim shoulder. She brightened, perking up. "And I'm glad I did. I love it here. It's so freeing."

To Charlotte, the only free thing here were the girls' bodies. They might all be dressed so cutely and sweetly, but there wasn't anything cute or sweet about the way their titties bounced. There was nothing nice about the way their bare asses hung out. By putting themselves on display and embracing whatever sick freedom they'd been influenced to believe in by Mamba, the girls were drastically devaluing themselves. Charlotte firmly believed that sex was not a thing that should come easily, or lightly. A man shouldn't be able to get a woman as easily as he could pick up a mint on the way out of a restaurant.

Kat glanced over her shoulder. "I need to go."

"Sure," Charlotte said quickly. "I didn't mean to keep you so long."

Kat stood up straight and held her arms close to her sides, pushing her bosom forward. "It was all my pleasure." The cat-girl jumped away from the table and scampered away, to a door near the back Charlotte hadn't noticed until right then.

Charlotte got up and went over to the bar. Other than the bouncer, the bartender behind the counter was the only working male in the entire establishment. At least that toxic, venomous Mamba sensed his girls might need occasional protection from the stronger sex.

"Excuse me," Charlotte said.

The bartender glanced in her direction. He was young, maybe in his mid-twenties, with long shaggy hair and a beard. His lack of a hairnet disgusted Charlotte almost as much as the length of his hair. Men might be more powerful than women, but they lacked sense. This guy had to be shedding hairs all over every item of food and every glass of drink he touched.

The bartender didn't respond right away. He wandered his eyes down Charlotte's body and then back up to her face, taking his time with it. She gasped softly with shock. She'd just been checked out, and with such uncouth casualness.

"Hey, pretty lady," the guy said, his voice smooth, though a bit reedy. "What can I get for you?"

Charlotte sat down on a bar stool, gripping the edges of her seat. She had to fight hard to restrain the urge to look at him like he was shit on her shoe, a piece of garbage on an immaculate floor. Men like him were the stains of society. They weren't real men, just the essence of them, composed of all the worst parts. But, she couldn't show him that. She had to play nice. "I had a question. Could you help me?"

He grinned and leaned over her, leering down at her from above. "I can do whatever you want, lady. What's up?"

"That's exactly the question I wanted to ask. What's up with this place? I've never known anywhere like it."

"Yeah, I don't doubt that." The bartender tapped his finger emphatically on the counter. "Lollipop is crazy. It's special. The owner, Mamba? The guy is like magic. He's got his fingers in everything. He must be like, crazy rich. I never met the guy, myself. Unless the guy I talked to for my interview was him, but I doubt it. Guy like Mamba, he'd never stoop so low to do stuff like that himself."

The poor guy had stars in his eyes as he talked. The enigmatic Mamba had him enchanted, entranced. The snake had turned the tide and charmed the charmers, manipulated them.

"Anyway, you look closely at anything that happens in this city and Mamba's involved somehow. Especially when it's about sex."

"Why?"

"You're kidding." The bartender broke out of his trance to turn a confused expression her way. "Sex sells. Sex influences. Sex is everything. Mamba gets the girls here by appealing to them with sex. Their own sex. He shows up to tons of high school graduations to speak on women's liberation. He says women should be able to do whatever they want. To hell with tradition! To hell with society!" He held out his arm, a sweeping gesture in the direction of the stage. "All those kittens and rabbits and little piglets come from pretty ordinary backgrounds. Then Mamba gets a hold of them and shows them how things can really be. They come here. They go on. And they never look back."

She couldn't listen any longer. Her mind hurt. Her soul hurt, being in this damn place. She pushed away from the bar and stumbled off blindly, not knowing where it was she was going.

Tradition? Society? Those were things she had valued her whole life. She'd been raised to believe women should marry and settle down when they were in the prime of their life. Their energy should go towards having children and raising the children, breastfeeding them and tending to their needs. A daycare center or a stay-at-home-dad wouldn't do as replacement. Everything she'd seen and heard and read told her that the traditional family unit was the best for society as a whole.

And Mamba was spitting his venom all over her beliefs.

"Hey. You. Red blouse."

Charlotte drew up short and looked around, knowing she was the only person in the vicinity wearing a blouse of any color. A man perhaps twice her age motioned her over to the stage. She looked over her shoulder at the exit, wanting nothing more than to leave.

"Psst," the older man hissed.

She had gone through too much already to have any sort of patience. Her control snapped. She stormed over to the man and demanded, "What?"

He leaned in close to her, bringing with him a scent of cologne and sweat and something musky. "I've seen you going around, asking questions."

She narrowed her eyes, held her tongue.

"Yeah, I thought so." He acted like she'd spoken anyway. "Listen, this stage? This front area? It's all a cover. The good stuff happens in the back."

She paused. "What do you mean, the good stuff?"

"How about you find out for yourself?" The man reached inside his vest. Charlotte tensed, but all he pulled out was a card. He held it out to her.

Charlotte took the card and looked at it. About the size and shape of a credit card, it was silver and had the letters V.I.P. on it. She turned it over and found the same on the other side. "What is this?"

"Take it. See that door back there?" The man nodded at the door Kat had gone through before. "Hold up the card in the air before you go through and the bouncer won't stop you."

Charlotte nibbled her lip. "Don't you need this?"

"I was going to hand it in, anyway. They hand them out to regulars. But," he shrugged, "my favorite girl is moving on to a new club after tonight and I got no more use for it. Might as well give it to you so you can get those answers you want."

This is a trap. Or it's not a trap and it's simply something I don't want to get caught up in.

Charlotte tried to give the card back. "I can't accept this."

The man put his hands in his pockets. "Then just drop it on a table or something. Geez. Just wanted to do a beautiful woman a favor."

He turned and sat back down in his seat. The lights started pulsing again, signaling the start of another routine.

Charlotte turned the card over and over in her hand. Here was her ticket to discovery. The question was if she wanted to board this particular train or not.

She knew what she had been asked to do. With the rug pulled out from underneath her, her expectations upended, she had only that to rely on.

Gripping the card, Charlotte went up to the unmarked, inconspicuous door. She held the card up over her head. The shiny plastic caught the light, reflected it. The bouncer must have seen, because he made no move to stop her.

Charlotte grabbed the doorknob and twisted, pushed inward. The door opened without a sound on greased hinges. The hallway in front of her was dark, impossibly dark. A smell wafted out of the black tunnel, steamy and thick and not unpleasant. She was unable to place the aroma. Drawn by curiosity, she stepped into the hall and shut the door behind her.

Lights snapped on at her approach, dull red, but startlingly bright in the void. A row of them led to a second door, which she opened and went through the same as the first.

The room before her was circular, with semicircular rows of chairs all facing several oversized pink couches. Sitting on those couches were naked girls, moaning and writhing in ecstasy as they used vibrators on themselves and each other. Their faces flushed red. Sweat covered their limbs, dripped between perky, heaving titties. Each girl with their legs spread wide to show off their wet, slippery folds, blossoming like wildflowers in exotic shades of coral and peach and rose.

As her eyes adjusted, Charlotte saw the chairs were occupied by men, sipping their drinks, talking among each other, and enjoying the crass display the girls were putting on for them.

She backed up, hit the closed door. Horror swelled inside her.

Now she recognized that smell.

It was the smell of immorality.

Chapter Three

Enough is enough

A MAN TURNED TO look in her direction. "Hey, pretty lady."

If someone called her that another time, she was going to scream.

"You here to join in the fun?"

Another man turned around, draped his arm over the back of the chair. "She's no dancer. You want a taste of the wild side, honey? Someone give this girl a turn on a controller."

"Controller?" Charlotte mouthed.

The first man tossed something at her. She flinched, throwing her arms in front of herself to catch the lobbed object. A slick device with two buttons. The On-button was obvious, while the other served to deepen her confusion. Something to do with speed?

"You gotta know what a vibrator is," the second man laughed aloud. "It's already on. Turn up the speed. See who you've got."

A shiver passed through her body and she nearly threw the thing across the room, right at the hapless girls wriggling around on the couch. They were all tangled up together, their limbs tossed together, forming a mass of sexual degradation. Their hair was tossed all over, draped over the back of the couch and sticking to their sweat-slicked bosom.

Charlotte's vision narrowed down to the size of a pin and her legs turned to noodles beneath her. She grabbed out at a chair and supported herself against it while the world whirled and spiraled around her. "I can't."

"Sure you can," the second man said. "You got a V.I.P. card. You can do anything you want. Just push the button. You'll be so glad you did."

Charlotte shook her head vehemently.

"Too much for her?" suggested a third man Charlotte couldn't see. Through the tunnel of her vision, all she could see was the girls on the couch. She couldn't take her eyes off of them.

"Push the button. You wouldn't be back here if you didn't want to."

A soft murmur ran through the room, a cultlike chanting imploring Charlotte to push the button, push the button, push the button. The cadence of the chant began to line up with the bucking and thrusting of the girls as they bucked on their various toys, writhed their hips around the objects buried inside them. It was all so hypnotizing.

Charlotte flexed her fingers around the remote, found the two buttons, slightly raised from the rest of the remote like nipples on a flat chest. Something sinister was going on here and it frightened her. The exterior cuteness combined with this sickening underbelly, and Mamba's involvement in the girls' lives. Mamba prepared them for this, inundated them with what he wanted to learn. He molded them like putty, played them like instruments.

Their lives were ruined.

How far did the ruination go? How deeply had Mamba corrupted them?

The controller in her hand had to be a prop to get the men to think they were involved. Charlotte could see no reason why even someone as cold-blooded and manipulative as Mamba would give that much power to his customers.

It's all about power. Giving men the power to use women as they see fit.

She had to know.

She could have wept from the dreadful curiosity filling her mind. She could have left at any time, but before she left she had to know how deep the rabbit hole went.

Like a hapless rodent wandering down a tunnel, knowing a predator awaited at the end, Charlotte found the speed button with her thumb. She pushed it. The remote buzzed in her hand, and again she almost threw it.

And then she did drop it, as one of the girls on the couch let out a piercing shriek. It was the girl in the direct middle of the couch. She grabbed the back of the couch with one hand and the cushion beneath her bared ass with the other. She lifted her ass up and thrust her pelvis forward, grinding on the air, thrusting herself on an invisible prick. Her slit jiggled, her entire vulva quivering from the force of the vibration coming from inside her. Rocking her head back, she let out another loud cry and continued to buck at the air.

"More!" the girl moaned. "More!"

Charlotte put her hand to her mouth, horrified, feeling like she had been punched in the stomach, stabbed in the eyes. She recognized that voice. She hadn't been able to tell from so far away, with all the girls being around the same age, with the same slutty silver-blonde hair, but that voice confirmed it. That deep, lusty yell came from the throat of Katerina, the cat-girl.

Murmurs of approval ran around the audience. Someone picked up the remote and put it in Charlotte's hand again, curling her fingers around it.

"More!" Katerina howled, practically out of her mind with her body's consuming need.

Charlotte groaned with horror and pushed the button again, for her research.

Katerina squealed and arched her back, her legs splayed wide so they crossed over the top of the legs of the girls on either side of her. Her labia was swollen, her nub engorged and erect. Every intricate detail of her inner crevices were on display, spread so far apart that Charlotte could even see the end of the vibrator buzzing around in her. Spasms went through the girl, making her limbs jump. Her tight muscles pulsated, clenched hard around the toy. She was an earthquake, an eruption of eagerness and impatience just waiting to happen.

Unable to stand any longer, Charlotte dropped down into the chair she'd been leaning on. She felt like weeping as she pushed the button again, sending the vibration speed rocketing up another notch. How many more were there left to cycle through until she came back to the initial setting, the lowest one?

Katerina dragged her nails on the material of the couch, leaving gouges. She began to thrust up and down, tits bouncing all over the place. Her eyes clenched shut, her mouth dragging open as gasps and groans pulsed from her throat. A trickle of saliva ran from the corner of her mouth; pleasure had rendered her near-comatose. Charlotte could tell the girl wasn't thinking, that it was only her body reacting to stimulus. She refused to believe anything else. No person in their right mind would go through such a thing. This level of sexual deviancy, the pleasure associated with it, it had to be excruciating and painful.

Her own sex organs twinged with sympathy for the poor girl.

Charlotte slammed her thumb on the button twice more in rapid succession, searching for the end of the cycle.

Katerina screamed and plunged both hands between her legs, sliding her fingers over lower lips, through her folds. She rubbed spasmodically, all fine motor control having escaped her.

In desperation, Charlotte pressed the button another time, but there seemed to be no end to how high the vibration could go.

"I'm gonna... ahh!" Katerina purred.

The girls on either side of her paid no attention to her yelling and writhing, all of them locked into similar experiences. The screaming and moaning was so loud, Charlotte had no idea how it couldn't be heard from outside. How could no one know about this? How could this be kept a secret?

Suddenly, Katerina snatched another vibrator that lay on the couch and turned it on, bringing it to her swollen nub. Now she was being vibrated from the inside and out, and there was no way her body could withstand the onslaught. The powerful lights in the room allowed for every moment of her orgasm to be seen. Wetness flowed over her lower lips, and a burst of her juice spattered against her inner thighs, dripping and smearing all over her smooth skin. Then, Katerina collapsed onto her back with her mouth open. She whimpered and squeaked as the vibrator inside her continued to work on her sensitive flesh.

Charlotte was shaking almost as much as her. She found the power button and pushed it.

Katerina finally lay still, limp, emptied.

For the first time in the past several minutes, Charlotte breathed, exhaling raggedly.

Katerina lifted her head and smiled at the crowd, a big and bright smile that showed she was so proud of herself for what she had done. It had to be a lie, a façade, but she was smiling anyway and it killed Charlotte's heart to see. "Who's turn is it now?"

Charlotte stood up, holding the remote control, thrusting it out at every man she saw. "Take this. Take this away from me. I can't do this any longer."

One of the men eagerly took it, turned it on right away, which made Katerina cry out with the joy she had been brain-washed into feeling.

Charlotte grabbed for the door, pulled herself to it and threw it open. She left it open behind her, the screams and moans from the room following her like she was escaping hell. She ran down the hallway and threw the second door open, and fell out into the main section of the club.

"Here," she said, and threw the silver V.I.P. card at the bouncer running over. He ignored her and dashed down the hall, shutting the door to the secret area. The voices of the oversexed girls were cut off in an instant.

There must be some insane soundproofing back there. My goodness.

Had she come on another day, she might have seen things even worse. Animal sacrifice. *An orgy.*

Charlotte got out of there as the bouncer headed back in her direction. This time, she had no qualms about leaving Lollipop, bursting out of the club and into the summer night. The air that touched her skin was thick, sticky, reminding her too much of the atmosphere in the secret back room. Shuddering and rubbing her arms, she ducked her head and went around the building to the back parking lot.

Finding her car, she pulled her keys out of her pocket and jammed them into the ignition. The entirely-innocent act now felt very sexual, very suggestive, and she hated it more than she could even express.

Charlotte turned the air-conditioning to full blast and leaned back in the driver's seat. The cold wind banished the disgusting warmth and helped her feel less flushed. Out in the dark, in the stillness of night, things felt more real, more solid. What had happened in the club already took on the haze of a nightmare.

She believed in privacy, as a rule. Certain things shouldn't be shared on for the world to see, and what happened in the bedroom between a couple should stay in the bedroom. Dreams and nightmares belonged in that category. People liked to talk about them, which forced others to listen out of politeness. No one cared about dream symbolism, or the funny thing that had happened, and no one wanted to hear about nightmares. Knowing what a co-worker feared was knowing too much about them, crossing a professional line.

However, this nightmare was an exception.

Her boss had wanted her to come out here and take a look around to see how things were. Oh, she had learned how things were, and she needed to share what she now knew with the world. She had to piece together these fragments of bad dreams and narrate them, because this fear she had gone through was one shared by many others. Only by starting a conversation about it could a solution be found.

Charlotte shifted her car into drive and pulled out–another suggestive action–of the parking lot. She drove onto a quiet side street and followed it until she came to the main road. Like most cities, this one was just as active at night, perhaps even more than during the daytime.

She joined a line of other vehicles at a red light, breaking a little too late and then really having to slam them on before she rear-ended the car in front of her. Her head snapped forward on her neck, snapped back. She rubbed the back of her neck with her hand and shut her eyes tight.

"Get it together," she whispered to herself, and smacked her own cheek lightly.

A car honked behind her. Opening her eyes, she saw the light had changed to green. She stepped on the gas and got to driving again, heading for the several skyscrapers in the near distance. Her company's building was part of that cluster.

She couldn't wait until tomorrow to go to her studio and make this video. Bad dreams faded. She couldn't let this fade. This warning, this call to action, it had to happen now while the memories lingered fresh.

What she would say or do, she didn't have figured out. All she knew was she couldn't settle for a simple fix, a treatment of the symptoms. No warm glass of milk or nightlight could banish the monster under the bed that was Mamba.

This required a direct attack.

Chapter Four

On the attack

CHAMPION MEDIA, THE COMPANY where Charlotte worked, looked much like any other office building on the outside. The difference was internal, both where the equipment and the employees were concerned. CM touted itself as a news source, an outlet for the unconventional. Where television news programs talked about politics and news websites touted the same boring articles over and over again, CM discussed the important things. Rights. Equality. Current Events across the globe.

The discussion didn't come just in the form of written words, or from people sitting down in front of a screen to recite from a teleprompter. Of course, CM also did those, but CM was on every platform: quick video, photo-sharing, and short messaging included. CM had its own publishing department, where books could be printed, and an art program. CM had everything.

Charlotte had everything at her disposal to take down Mamba, and she planned to use all of it.

Charlotte stepped out of her car and hurried into the air-conditioned lobby. A security guard glanced up at her arrival and frowned. "ID?"

"Are you serious? I work here."

"Either you show me some ID, or you flash them titties," the guard said, grinning at his own slant rhyme.

His words were like a slap to the face. Charlotte reared her head back and stared at him, memorizing his face so she could report him for harassment. "You..." She sputtered. "You ignorant man."

The guard kept grinning. "Don't you know that things have changed around here?"

"I wasn't aware," she said haughtily, planting her hands on her hips. She had bigger things to deal with than this little lizard who thought he was a snake. "And I don't give a damn. You want my ID? Fine. Here." She reached for her wallet.

The man waved his hand and turned away, going back to the front desk to pick up the magazine he'd been reading before she came in and interrupted him. To her dismay, she saw it was a porn mag. A woman bent over, spreading her ass cheeks for a black man with an anaconda "Whatever," the guard said. "I don't have time to waste on you. You're no threat."

"You wouldn't recognize a threat if someone came and pointed a gun at your head!" Charlotte said. "Sitting there like that, looking at those horrible pictures. Your brains have been rotted!"

He shrugged and sat down, kicking up his boots to rest them on the desk. Charlotte hurried past, and heard him pull down his zipper. She didn't dare look back, not that she needed to know what he was about to do. The receptionists who came in and sat in that chair during the day would never know how filthy their space was, how soiled by the desires of a degenerate male.

Charlotte jabbed the button for the elevator and hopped inside. She spun and slapped the button for her floor. The doors closed and the elevator hummed, vibrating its way up the tower. She staggered back and rested on the wall, head tilted up to stare at the single bright light fixture overhead.

She had CM's resources at hand. This late at night, she wouldn't have to deal with anyone else and explain her actions. She should have been feeling better than this. She was still just so shaken by what she'd seen. She felt dirty for having played a part in the debauchery, no matter how small.

I'll make it right, she told herself. *I'll make up for it.*

The elevator doors opened and she stepped out onto her floor, floor 12, affectionately known as the Stage. Every door she passed led to a filming studio, some little bigger than closets, others the size of a television newsroom. All the rooms on the other side of the doors were dark, locked up due to the late hour, the creators all having gone home. However, during the day, the stars, producers, and cameramen would come and capture pure, unadulterated content to send off to teams of editors. The editors would create videos from the raw footage, then send the drafted videos to carefully selected watchers. The watchers watched. That was their whole job. The watchers gave comments and feedback, which a second round of editors applied to the videos before finally sending them off to be uploaded.

The streamlined process ensured CM put out a steady stream of videos, which had them constantly trending. Some of the videos were entire skits and short films written by in-house writers, and others were game shows with high production value.

Some people, like Charlotte, worked by themselves as singular, relatable creators meant to target an extremely specific audience.

Charlotte let herself into her filming studio and turned on the lights. She shut and locked the door behind her. The door was heavy, padded thickly with soundproofing, a similar treatment of which had been given to the walls. All the studios had the same preventions in place to ensure the creators didn't bother each other. The members of the audience, too, were to be kept in the dark. Damian wanted the world to think that each of the creators were independent, and not all part of this one monolithic organization.

The chubby 32-year-old man in the room next to Charlotte's played RPGs and recorded the content. His room was made to look like a simple bachelor's living room, with some cheap lighting and a moderately expensive microphone. An entire backstory had been created for him, a life which other departments in CM had brought to life through social media.

Across the hall, an old woman in baggy clothes made quick, snappy videos, eccentric videos always relating to trendy topics. She was made to seem like a bit of a hermit, lovable and slightly crazy, a bumbling grandmother who didn't have any real idea how she'd gotten into this video thing. In actuality, she was a retired psychologist who used her skills to craft her scripts and visuals.

It was all a façade. Many clever façades.

Charlotte participated in her own façade so often she felt like an entirely different person while filming. When she entered her studio, the rest of her fell away, leaving behind the concentrated essence of an auntlike figure. A bit old-fashioned, but friendly, endearing, and always wanting what was best for the next generation.

But she didn't feel like that today. She still felt like herself.

Charlotte stepped deeper into her room and sighed, softly. Her studio had been made to look like a classy unmarried woman's bedroom. She filmed herself sitting on the big bed, perched on the red duvet with black and white pillows at her back. A nightstand with a quirky-looking black lamp was always in the background of the shot; as the seasons changed, she would set up different decorations there.

Other fixtures in the room were her makeup table, and the chair on the other side of the room where she reviewed books she had read–nearly always self-help books for young adults.

A second door next to the makeup table led to her dressing room, though her viewers believed it to be a connected bathroom.

Charlotte went over to the other door and touched the knob. She jerked her hand back like she'd been shocked. Rubbing her hands together, she paced.

In there, she had appropriate outfits and props to fit the persona she wore. She always touched up her makeup and did her hair in there, and whatever else she needed to do for the day.

If she did that today, if she went along with her routine, viewers might believe this was an ordinary video. Never before had she lied to her impressionable audience.

The reason she was here right now was because she couldn't bring herself to lie to them, no matter what her boss wanted.

Charlotte turned away from the door, putting her back to it. "It'll be like when those problematic beauty gurus make apology videos," she whispered. "And they wear baggy clothes and no makeup. It'll be a sign something isn't right."

It was a good idea.

She knew what she was about to do was a good idea.

There was no point in wasting more time thinking about it.

Charlotte went over to the corner of the room where she kept her filming supplies and set up her camera. Going through the practiced motions she knew so well helped her to feel better. Not much, but enough to steady her hands and harden her resolve. This was what had to be done and she would do it.

With the camera set up and recording, Charlotte went and sat down in her usual spot on the bed. Rather than lounge back or cross her legs like she normally would, she found herself folding her hands in her lap and leaning forward.

"Hi everyone," she said softly, softer than she normally would. "And welcome back to Living, Loving, Lifestyling, the most positive and encouraging channel you'll ever come across. I'm your host, Charlotte. Here at Triple L, we're all about making dreams come true. Whether it's learning a new skill or asking out that boy you're interested in, I'm here to give you advice on it. You know I'm always honest with you and I always act with the best of intentions."

Charlotte swallowed hard. This was difficult. Fortunately, with the intro out of the way, she could get on to what she really wanted to talk about.

"I tell you what I think, what I like, what I don't like. I give you recommendations, and I tell you things I think you should avoid. Unfortunately, that's what we're here to talk about today. I went somewhere today under the assumption I was going to have a positive experience and instead, I ended up feeling sick and betrayed. I cannot, in all good conscience, be silent about what I saw and what I went through."

Though I will be silent about my involvement. That's my burden alone.

"I went to a place called Club Lollipop tonight. I was told I'd learn something there about a different kind of work, one I've always said I disapprove of. That's right, I'm talking about sex work. Club Lollipop is a strip club. The young women who work there are just a little older than most of you who will watch this, but they all dress up like children. Cute dresses, animal ears, and tails. I didn't understand it and I didn't want to go, but I know I can be wrong sometimes. I know because you always call me out in the comments." She forced a dry chuckle. "I wanted to see if I really could learn something from my visit to the club. And I did learn. I learned a very terrible truth that I have to share with all of you so you'll be safe.

"Club Lollipop is nothing more than a front. It's evil wearing a cute mask. The girls who work there are selected before they're even old enough, chosen by the club's owner, a man I know only as Mamba."

Her voice trembled on his name.

"Mamba chooses these girls because they're pretty and he wants to use them. He manipulates them, implants them with suggestions and ideas to get them to work for him. He guides them to his club so he can take advantage of them. It's brainwashing. By the time they've graduated high school, these girls don't know anything else except what Mamba has put in their heads. Those young women I saw could be at college or moving up in the world, making names for themselves. Instead, they're put in cute costumes and treated like toys. Nameless toys. It's awful.

"And I know what you're asking. Where's my proof? I talked to several people who worked there and they all told me what I just told you. I'm sure if I had taken pictures or video, I would have been thrown out. I couldn't risk it. I had to be sure for myself. And I am sure. Club Lollipop is not a good place. It isn't sweet or nice or a good work opportunity. It's a gateway to degeneracy and a life of destitution. Club Lollipop is bad. Mamba is bad. I wish I could say otherwise, but there's just no way around it."

She ran out of breath and stopped, her lungs quivering inside her. "I'm sorry this video is short and serious, but you needed to know. I love all of you and I wanted to protect you. I'll see you next time on Triple L. Until then, please, stay safe, and stay away from people who make promises that are too good to be true. Because they are."

The words ran out and she sat there afterward for a moment, trying to think of anything else she could add. Eventually, she shook her head and got up, and turned off the camera. She pulled out the memory card and stuck it into her pocket.

Charlotte walked up to the door to leave. She stood in front of the soundproof foam cubes and wondered if she really was brave enough to go through with this. It would be going against Damian. Against her boss. It was a direct attack. She'd lose her job.

"So be it," she whispered, and stepped out into the hall. What Mamba was doing was a direct attack on women everywhere. She had to retaliate. If that made her a martyr, then so be it.

Back in the elevator, she went up another two floors to reach the Cutting Room, where dozens of editors slaved for hours to put videos together from raw footage. This part of CM resembled a real office more than any other area, set up like a typical cubicle land, though with two and three high-tech monitors instead of one. Even now, at such a late hour, there were a few editors hard at work, watching the same fragments of footage for the hundredth time.

"There's coffee," someone muttered, barely taking the time to register her presence.

"Thanks."

No response.

Charlotte sat down at one of the terminals and booted it up, and typed in her username and password. No one had a permanent seat out here in the Cutting Room, though some people did tend to sit in the same spots. The thin walls and desk in her terminal were clean, white, boring. The absence of color and distractions had always been soothing to her. Now, already uneasy, the blankness put her on edge.

Stuck out here to perform at the hands of our superiors. Is there a difference between CM and Lollipop?

Charlotte fed the memory card into the computer and pulled the footage into an editing program. Yes, she decided, there was a difference. Talented and willing adults worked at CM. Lollipop targeted those who were just starting out in the world, ensnaring them from their first steps from shelter.

In the editing program, Charlotte clipped out the beginnings and endings of her footage, considering it unprofessional to be seen turning the camera on and off. Otherwise, her videos never had jump cuts or special effects, nothing of the kind. The simplicity meant she could do it herself in ten minutes and then send it off to Damian for approval. Once he approved, he'd post it.

He hadn't ever disapproved before.

She'd just cut out the middle man this time and do it herself.

Having saved her video, she went over and logged into her video channel's account. She loaded up the video and since it was so short, barely a few minutes long, it was ready right away. Charlotte added a title, "What You Need to Know About Club Lollipop," and added in a short, vague description asking viewers to watch right to the end. After that, there was nothing to do. The video was too short to monetize or insert ads. She wouldn't have done so anyway. She didn't want CM making money off of a warning, an alarm.

Charlotte hovered the mouse cursor over the upload button and closed her eyes. She searched deep inside herself to figure out if this was truly what she wanted. She had no doubts though, not a single one. Nodding to herself, she opened her eyes and clicked to upload.

Charlotte sat back in her chair, breathing out a sigh of... resignation? Relief? She didn't know. But it was done. She couldn't take it back. As she sat there, a notification popped into her account's inbox. Someone in her large audience had been awake at this hour and already clicked the video, already finished watching. She went to look at the notification and in the time it took her screen to refresh, one had turned into five. Likes, shares, and comments.

"WOW I didnt know this," read one.

Another: "I think I've heard of this guy. I had no idea he was so pervy. Thanks, Triple L, for always watching out for us."

Another page refresh showed now tens, dozens of comments flooding in. The like counter on her video ticked up rapidly, and her logistics page showed her it was being shared to at least three other platforms at that point.

She didn't want to watch anymore. She'd done what she knew she should and the truth was out there.

Charlotte logged off the computer. She stood up and gathered up her purse.

One of the other workers glanced over in her direction. "That was quick. Lucky. Mine needs quirky special effects every few seconds or he looks insane."

They thought she was another editor, didn't recognize her as the diamond play button-star she was. Her heart lodged in her throat. They'd remember her tomorrow, though. When Damian came asking.

"I just had to clean up the ending," she said.

"Lucky," the other worker repeated. They went back to looking down at their computer.

Clutching her purse tightly to her side, Charlotte hurried to get out of there before she attracted any more attention to herself.

Chapter Five

You're nothing

HER EYES POPPED OPEN and she sat up with a cry of anguish lodged in her throat. Her breasts heaved under her cream nightgown, a demure shift that went right down to her knees. Charlotte drew up her legs to her chest, compressing her breasts so she felt her nipples through the fabric. She hugged herself and tried to catch her breath, darting glances around the room.

Golden morning sunlight spilled through the drawn curtains, turning them from soft lavender to amber. The glow spread far across her small, tidy bedroom, chasing the shadows back to the corners. And to behind the closet door, under the bed, where children believed monsters lived.

Charlotte untangled herself from her sheets and crept over to the edge of her bed on her hands and knees. She bent over and peered into the gap underneath, searching for the creature that had haunted her dreams the whole night. Shadows coiled beneath the bed, sinuous, snakelike, so that for a moment she gasped and flinched, expecting fangs to dart out of the darkness and slice into her throat. She could even picture the blank, ebony eyes, locked onto her, seeing her for the prey she was.

She backed away from the bed and lifted her head, blood rushing away from her face. The change in position left her dizzy. She shook her head to clear it, trying to dislodge the impossible nothing from her mind.

You are being childish, Charlotte, she scolded herself. *There is nothing under there. And if there is, it's a mouse. At worst, a rat. Or a freaking garden snake. Someone's escaped pet. But more than likely, there's nothing under there.*

She put her knuckles to her lips, pressing hard enough to mash them painfully to her teeth. Swallowing hard, she bent over for another look. This time, as she descended, she realized how sexual of a position it was to be on all fours with her ass in the air. She was asking for some masked intruder to come in and jump on her.

Another ridiculous notion, but she was full of them that morning.

Charlotte flattened herself out so she lay on her stomach. Even that didn't feel quite right, so she grabbed her blankets and tossed them over her lower half.

Better.

She no longer had anything to distract her from what she was meant to be doing. Charlotte thrust her head down the side of the bed and peered upside-down into the shadows.

With the light in the room strengthening, the shadows were pushed back further, gray and faint against the wall. What she had mistaken for a reptile's eye was nothing more than a balled sock. Dust bunnies and cobwebs clung to the wall. Unthreatening. Benign. Everything was as it should have been.

Charlotte rolled out of bed onto the floor and fished the sock out from under the bed. It had been purple once—purple was her favorite color and she tried to incorporate it into every outfit—though a thick and fuzzy coat of dust obscured much of the fabric. "Ugh," she said, disgusted, and tossed the sock into a little trash bin she kept in the corner of the room. She regretted it as soon as she did. Little tufts of dust blew off the sock and floated around the room, glowing like jewels in the morning light.

"Ugh," she said again. She stood up, dusting off her hands. Filth bothered her. Filth of all kinds.

That brought her back to what she had done last night and what was no doubt the reason for her terrifying dreams.

Anxiety knotted her stomach. She put her hands over her middle and rubbed herself, stroking in circles to soothe her worry. There was nothing to be done for it now. She'd have to live with what she'd done.

"No point going in to work," she said aloud, tasting the words. They tasted of defeat. She tried again. "I did what I had to. It cost me my job, so there's no point in going to work."

That felt a little bit better. She couldn't sit passively by. She had to take actions, even if those actions were small.

What did martyrs do after they had martyred themselves? The ones who hadn't yet died for their cause, that was.

They wouldn't mope around and be sad, or let monsters under the bed scare them. They went on, knowing things would never be the same. They faced the consequences of their actions. So, she should face hers. She needed to look at her video channel account and judge the reaction. No doubt there would be articles written on her by now. Perhaps Mamba, or CM, had issued a statement. She had to find out what was being said so she could plan her next move.

Charlotte left her bedroom and crossed the hall to her office. Here, she paid her taxes, researched trends, and answered comments on her videos on her own time. Today she would be finding out her fate. She entered the room, which smelled of apples and cinnamon, and pulled the chair out from the desk. She started to sit down.

Was she ready for this?

The question came out of the blue and stopped her in her tracks. She still wore her pajamas. Her hair wasn't done. She hadn't eaten or had anything to drink, or even brushed her teeth. She was a mess. As a mess, could she make informed opinions and plan her next actions? Of course not.

Charlotte let go of her chair and went back out of the room, shutting the door behind her. She headed down the hall to her living room. Ignoring the television, her personal laptop, her charged phone, she passed through to the kitchen and put the coffee pot on. The delicious, earthy odor of coffee filtered around the room in an instant, a comforting ghost to haunt her wherever she went.

With the coffee brewing, Charlotte went over to the fridge and fetched eggs. The carton felt light, reminding her that she needed to buy more. In fact, she would do well to stock up on groceries now, while she still had money. She'd soon need to be frugal so she could afford to keep living in her apartment while hunting for another job.

Charlotte set butter to melting in a pan and started to crack eggs for her usual breakfast of egg whites on toast. She believed a dose of healthy protein and starch and just a bit of calorific fat was the best way to start the day. She'd done plenty of research on the subject and had conducted her own experiments using herself as the guinea pig until she found what worked best for her. She'd been having this exact same breakfast every day for five years now, even on holidays, even when she was sick and the idea of eating was enough to send her running for the toilet. If she felt a little adventurous, she might even sprinkle some salt and pepper on top of her eggs.

Charlotte finished separating out the first egg white and made to toss the yellow yolk in the garbage. She hesitated with the goopy mess dangling right over the trash can.

Maybe I should celebrate while I can.

She'd stuck up for what she believed in. For once in her life, she should treat herself.

Charlotte brought the yolk back over to her bowl and added it in. For the first time, she used two whole eggs instead of just the whites. It felt like a pitiful change. She added in a third before dumping them all in the pan together. And then she added salt and pepper right away.

But it still felt pitiful, like a child's attempt at rebellion. Look at her, coloring the sky red instead of blue. She was still staying in the lines.

Returning to the fridge, she scrounged around for something to make her morning truly different. She had a lot of things she used sparingly, cheeses and meats to add to her dishes. Now she dug those out and added generous portions to her cooking eggs, scrambling them all together until the eggs were done. The mess looked positively disgusting, super fatty and greasy. She brought it and a cup of coffee over to her table and ate every last bite, and drained her coffee down to the last sip.

Charlotte leaned back in her chair and put her hands on her stomach, feeling bloated from all the food inside her. She'd probably regret it later on but for the moment, she was sated.

She had celebrated.

It was a pitiful celebration to be sure, lacking alcohol or drugs like other people used when they wanted to have fun.

She wondered, for the first time, if she was boring.

She shook her head and left the table, again passing by her computer and phone, the devices that connected her to reality. She pulled clothes from the dresser in her room and headed into the shower to get cleaned up. She pulled her nightgown over her head, freeing her bosom. The cold atmosphere of the bathroom, with its porcelain features and tiled floor, made her nipples harden. She ignored the tingle that passed through her and pulled her panties down and kicked them to the side.

Naked now, in the safety of her own home, she stepped into the shower and turned on the water to a steamy blast. Hot water needled her skin, stinging her nipples and sliding down to scald the protruding outer lips of her femininity. She gasped, half in pain, half in delight at the cleansing heat. Ducking in and out of the spray, she washed her hair, spending more time scrubbing and massaging her scalp than she normally would to pamper herself. She left the conditioner in to let it sink into her dark brown locks and grabbed her bath pouf from where it hung on the corner shower stand. She poured a liberal amount of shower gel on the pouf and ran it over her body, from between her breasts all the way to the top of her mound, leaving a smear of white suds that the water sent running between her legs and to her feet.

The feel of silky foam gliding down her body gave her shivers. Charlotte wiggled her toes in the tide of soap on the shower floor. She kept washing, running the soft mesh folds over every inch of her body. Her arms, her breasts, her legs and feet. It felt so good that, when she was done, she couldn't help sliding her hand down to the apex of her thighs. She cupped her sex in the palm of her hand, felt her oversized lips sliding between her spread fingers. She probed with her middle finger, pushing through her soapy labia to the cusp of her entrance.

And there she stopped. Pulling her hand away from herself, she resumed showering, rinsing the suds from herself as if nothing had happened. Self-pleasure was a useful tool to help girls become familiar with their bodies. She advocated it in very small amounts, so young women could learn what to expect from their male partners. It was a learning process and not something to be taken lightly, or overused for the purpose of escaping reality.

She had nothing left to learn from her own body. She'd just gotten a little carried away, that was all. It was a little treat for herself, like her oversized breakfast. All that meat.

Charlotte finished her shower and stepped out to dry off, patting her body down. She dressed in a purple blouse and jeans, comfortable clothes that were like armor in their familiarity.

After brushing her teeth, she finally, finally felt as if she was ready to take on her newfound responsibility.

Charlotte held her head high while going into her office. She sat in her chair with her back straight and her shoulders squared, like a warrior ready to do battle. She ignored the tremor of uncertainty in the pit of her stomach, the quivering of nausea that made her want to throw up her breakfast.

Charlotte pulled up the video site and typed in the title of her video. Results poured in and she made to click on the first one, the one with the most views. The thumbnail made her stop. It was an image of a kid holding a lollipop. It should have been an autogenerated image of Charlotte herself. Unless YouTube had implemented some sort of weird thumbnail-generating algorithm...

No. She took another look at the title and realized it was indeed about lollipops. The candy kind.

Okay, she told herself, *so my video isn't popular enough to have become the number one search result.*

It wasn't in the second spot, either. In fact, as she scrolled, she couldn't find herself anywhere.

Weird, considering she'd searched for her exact title. This wouldn't be the first time the site had made a blunder with its search results, though.

Rather than continue poking around at random, she decided to just go straight to her channel. She typed in Living, Loving, Lifestyling, and pressed enter.

No results.

The results weren't ones she didn't want. There were none at all. The site didn't recognize that particular combination of words.

"What is going on?" Charlotte demanded. She tried a search for Triple L, her channel's nickname, which again brought her to a bunch of results that didn't have anything to do with her. Her heart started beating faster. Something was wrong.

Charlotte went to the log-in page and typed in her username and password.

The video site didn't recognize her existence. Words in red told her there was no such username.

So, she had made a typo.

Charlotte used one trembling finger to tap out her login details one letter and number at a time. She made sure every keystroke was exactly correct, and pressed enter again.

Nothing.

Her channel had been deleted.

That was the only explanation. According to the site, she didn't exist. All of her was gone. Her channel, her videos. Years of work, eviscerated overnight.

Her heart thudded so fast she couldn't catch a breath. She put her hand over her mouth and squeezed her eyes shut, fighting for some semblance of control. Video sites had a system in place. Channels weren't just deleted. She had to get channel strikes, which she would have a chance to appeal. Maybe her channel and videos had merely been hidden. If she appealed...

Charlotte went to her email and logged in. Rather, tried to log in. The login rejected her, just as the video site had.

"No!" she cried. She tried again and again, the screen flashing and denying her every time. Charlotte slammed the enter button over and over and then bashed her fist on the keyboard.

She felt like she was dying inside, like her heart was on the verge of exploding, it was beating so fast. Surely, she couldn't take this strain for much longer. She couldn't outlast this.

Maybe my personal email.

Nothing.

But that couldn't be right. Her personal email wasn't connected to her work in any way. Her boss didn't even have it!

She tried the social network, the photo-sharing app all to the same result, or lack of it.

Tears brimmed in her eyes. Quickly running out of options, she resorted to the search engine. There would still be some trace of her, surely.

Charlotte typed in her channel's name.

The search engine gave her results for Live, Love, Laugh signs, and family blogs that had nothing to do with her.

Charlotte cried out again, her sob echoing in her office. Now entirely desperate, she entered her own full name and ran the search.

She'd made waves on the Internet for her content. She was on CM's website. She'd done interviews about her jobs and beliefs. She'd gone to school, been part of clubs that made appearances in newspapers. She even knew for a fact that her birth was online, because her father and mother were notable figures in the city before their deaths in a plane crash ten years ago.

But there was nothing.

According to the search engine, she hadn't ever even been born.

"Oh, my god," she whispered, rocking back in her chair. Despair gripped her tight. "Oh, my god!"

Was this legal?

It couldn't be.

She had to fight it.

Her heartbeat thudded in her ears. Loud, hollow.

Not her heartbeat, she realized. Someone was pounding on the door to her apartment, unceasingly.

"I'm coming," she called, pushing back from her desk. She stood up and staggered out of the room on legs that felt numb.

The pounding continued and even seemed to be getting louder, more fervent.

"I'm *coming!*" she cried, and unlocked the door and threw it open. "What?" she snapped.

A man with close-cropped hair stood in front of her door, hands clasped in front of himself. "Are you Charlotte Aria?" he asked. His voice was clipped, professional.

"Yes."

The man unclasped his hands and held out a letter to her, which she hadn't noticed before. "This is for you."

Charlotte took the letter. The envelope was plain and white, with her name and address on the outside. No return address had been given, presumably because it had been sent by courier and not through the mail. "What is this?"

The man gazed at her coolly, expressionless. "That is a summons to court."

"What?"

He misunderstood her shock for ignorance. "You are being sued, Ms. Aria."

Charlotte shut the door in his face and went into the bathroom to vomit.

Chapter Six

Bite back

CHARLOTTE SAT ON HER couch and read the court summons. The language was very dry and difficult to follow. She took notice of the important details. Firstly, that her court date was in only a week. In a city so large, that should have been impossible. Nothing happened as fast as this because there were hundreds of thousands, millions of other people all doing the same things. There had to be murder trials, divorce settlements, fraud cases ongoing all around this same time. She hadn't killed or done anything so terrible, so why should she get such special treatment?

But, of course, she had her answer thanks to the rest of the letter.

She was being sued by the owner of Lollipop on charges of defamation. And the person suing her was also the CEO of Champion Media.

Now she knew.

Now she knew why the new owner of CM had wanted her to work on such terrible videos.

Mamba owned CM.

And she had gone and targeted the very operation she was meant to be supporting. She had gone and upset a very, very powerful man who owned a *media company*. No wonder she had been wiped from the face of the planet. No wondering how, either. Everything Mamba needed to erase her was right there in the building, on one floor or another.

"What am I going to do?" she whispered.

The answer was obvious, however. She had to fight back. If she just sat around and accepted her fate, that would be the end of her. Mamba would send her to jail, drive her into poverty with fees. She had done what she believed in and letting him do that to her would be like admitting she was wrong, which she absolutely wasn't.

Charlotte leaned over and grabbed her phone, which she had neglected to look at thus far. She turned it on and checked for notifications. There were practically none, which she shouldn't have been surprised about, but which hit her like a load of bricks anyway. She still had all her usual apps on her phone, but she no longer existed on any of them. The only notifications left were those of text messages. One from Damian, and several from people she'd been close to at CM.

The message from Damian was quick, snappy. He had fired her and would be sending her last paycheck in the mail. She wasn't allowed back in the building.

The others were a mixed bag of disapproval and plain astonishment at what she had done.

Rather than answer any of them, she went straight to Google and looked up lawyers in her area. She called the best one she could reasonably expect to afford–by digging into her savings–and waited for thirty minutes while listening to hold music.

The hold music cut out. A woman with a rasping voice answered. "Lila Fredericks speaking. Please state your name and your business. I'm very busy at the moment."

"Ms. Fredericks," Charlotte said, aware of how pitiful her polite tone was in comparison to the lawyer's rasp, "my name is Charlotte Aria. I..."

"I'm going to stop you right there, Miss Aria. I know what you want and I'm not going to represent you."

"What?" Surely she hadn't heard right. "I haven't even said anything. I can pay you. I can pay double."

"No amount of money in the world is worth going up against that man. He would eat me alive. And he is going to eat you alive, Miss Aria." The lawyer suddenly spoke softer, gentler. "I don't know what your motivation was for this. I'm not heartless, but I have to protect myself. I doubt anyone in or out of this city will go up against him. You'd be much better off saving yourself the time and effort and just accepting a public defender right now. I can forward you to one."

"But..."

"You won't win this case. In my professional opinion, you want to use this time formulating a plan of how to minimize the damage he's going to inflict upon you."

Charlotte repeated, voice breaking, "I can pay double."

"No." Fredericks suddenly began to recite a series of digits. A phone number. "Did you get that? That's the number you'll call. If you ask for them to represent you, the courts have to allow it. I'm sorry. My daughter used to watch your videos. She made me watch that last one with her. I appreciate what you tried to do, but for my own safety, I can't have any part in it. Good luck."

"Triple!" Charlotte cried, breaking, but she was speaking to no one. The lawyer had hung up on her.

Charlotte pushed her fingers to the bridge of her nose, shaking. She hadn't anticipated this. She should have. She'd just thought that because all traces of her had been removed from online, no one would know yet. Mamba had been several steps ahead of her on that. He'd no doubt reached out to every high-profile lawyer and given them reason not to represent her.

But there had to be someone, didn't there? He couldn't have reached out to every single lawyer in the city.

He must have connections I don't even know about, though. He wiped me off the face of the planet. I'm insane to think that he isn't capable of contacting every lawyer out there.

She had to try.

She spent the rest of that day calling number after number. As the day wore on, secretaries started turning her away, or she had her calls outright ignored. Word was spreading. It was too late. She kept trying though, long after offices had closed for the day, making pleas to emotionless voicemail recordings. She slept only when exhaustion claimed her sometime after midnight.

The first pale gray fingers of dawn pushing through the slats of her blinds woke her. She got straight back to work with calling lawyers and attorneys, though now no one was answering her calls at all.

She had been blacklisted.

Hunger drove her to break away around noon. She went into the kitchen to grab some crackers and peanut butter and was making herself a plate when another knocking came at her door. Charlotte jumped, and dropped her plate. Porcelain shards flew all over the kitchen floor and peanut butter crackers went skidding underneath counters and the stove.

"Damnit," she said, and stepped over the mess. Something sharp jabbed at her heel, showing that she hadn't been entirely successful in her attempt. She ignored the pain and limped the rest of the way to the door.

Just as she arrived, the knocking ceased.

Charlotte hesitated, then threw the door open. No one stood there, though when she craned her head around to look, she noticed a letter had been left on the carpet. She picked it up and read it while standing in the doorway, leaning heavily on the frame.

It was a reminder of the summons, and a warning. She needed to contact the court with her lawyer by 6 p.m. tomorrow, or else she would be given the most available public defender automatically.

She went back into her apartment and sat on her couch, letting the mess sit in the kitchen. She was so ruined, so done for. Nothing could possibly help her now.

You have no choice. Call that number Lila Fredericks gave you.

Charlotte put her hand over her mouth and let out a soft, bitter little laugh. She went to clean up her mess in the kitchen and noticed little splotches of blood, a trail where she had stepped on a shard of plate and cut herself. She knew that would likely not be the only injury she sustained for this.

After she tossed the bloody, peanut buttery broken plate in the garbage, she went to make what she hoped–and dreaded–would be her final call.

A brisk, masculine speaker answered. "I hoped I'd hear from you."

"Is this..." Damn, she didn't even know their name.

"Link Parskey. Lila told me you might reach out, Charlotte. There's not much time to waste here. We need to meet."

This wasn't what she had expected. "Shouldn't we talk first? More than this, I mean?"

"No. I don't trust the phone, not when I know who you're going up against. Who we are going up against. Come to my office. 1454 North Boulevard. Come alone and come fast." Link hung up the phone before she could even say anything.

Charlotte knew she had no choice except to do as he asked. She got dressed and left her apartment building.

A reporter came scampering up to her as soon as she left the lobby. "Hi, Charlotte Aria, I'm Bethany Hamilton with..."

"No comment," Charlotte said, turning her head away from the woman. She walked faster, trying to get away.

The reporter followed, her heels clicking on the concrete. She thrust her arm forward, pushing her brown wrist past Charlotte so that the microphone she held was in front of her face. "News of your YouTube video is everywhere by now. Some people are calling you a traitor to your sex. Don't you have anything to say about that?"

She did, but she saved it all through her escape, and all through the long drive to Parskey's office. He was there to meet her, a mid-50s and balding gentleman in a suit that stretched a bit tight over his paunch. Parskey offered her his hand.

Charlotte burst out, "A traitor to my sex? I did this to defend my sex! I did this for the greater good of a younger generation!"

Link Parskey let his hand drop. "We aren't here to discuss whether what you did was right or wrong, Charlotte. We're here to make a plan. You won't win this case. We need to minimize the damage."

She tossed her arms into the air and turned away from him, glaring out at the packed street. "That's exactly what that Lila woman said to me."

"I'm not surprised, considering that she's my sister," Parskey said dryly. "We tend to think alike. Unfortunately for you, so does everyone in the city right now. Come back here with me so we can talk privately. Would you like something to drink?"

"Water."

Parskey chuckled, leading her through the lobby to a wide and somewhat romantic office, filled with dark oak furniture and lined with bookcases. "Normally when I ask that question, people want alcohol."

Charlotte accepted the bottle of water handed to her and sat down in a chair in front of the impressive oak desk. "I barely ever drink. I think all vices should be eliminated or taken with extreme conservation."

Parskey sat down behind his desk and looked at her in a way she didn't quite like. "You're a woman of strong beliefs. Conservative beliefs, if I can borrow the word you just used."

She nodded, sitting up straighter and lifting her chin. "It's how I was raised."

"Sometimes, it's wise to reevaluate what we think we know. But of course, it's too late for that now. Let's do some damage control, Charlotte." Parskey opened up a laptop and looked at her hard. Do you want to plead guilty or not guilty to the accusations?"

"Not guilty."

"Of course. So we need an explanation for the way you acted. Tell me what happened and we'll see what plausible defense we can find in the truth."

"Why not just tell the truth?" she asked.

Parskey gave her another dark look. "You already told the truth and look where that got you. Start explaining, Charlotte."

So she told him everything from the very beginning and over the next several days, Parskey crafted a line of defense for her. He would make her out to be a sheltered bachelorette from a conservative background, a vulnerable and relatively innocent woman very much in line with her online persona. She had been misguided by her strong beliefs and made a mistake. That would be Parskey's selling point, that a mistake had been made. She wasn't the only person to ever mess up while in the spotlight. She hadn't done anything intentionally wrong, though in the heat of the moment she had definitely violated her contract and said some heated things in the process.

She was almost impressed by it. He had really taken the truth and spun it to her advantage. Had she been hearing this about another woman, she would have supported her. For a public defender, Link Parskey had talent. Her last line of defense was as good as it could be.

Her first court date arrived and it was a media circus. News vans clustered the street outside the courthouse, and reporters and journalists flooded the sidewalks. They shouted their questions at Charlotte. She didn't answer any of them. Parskey and a number of police officers held the ravenous newshounds at bay, but there was an even bigger enemy to contend with.

Everyone in the city knew what she had said and done. Mamba, with his terrible influence, had twisted the story in his favor, and now droves of young adults had gathered at the courthouse to act upon what they had been led to believe. They shouted at Charlotte, repeating the phrase that had become so common by now, that she was a traitor to her sex. They called her old-fashioned, a grandmother, a boomer, a misogynist, and waved signs in her direction. And sex workers had emerged, prostitutes from the streets and strippers from their clubs, telling her she was outdated and doing more harm than good by slut-shaming and denying the dignity of their jobs.

By the time she got inside the air-conditioned cool of the courthouse, she was shaking. The world had turned upside-down. She had gone from being so loved to so hated. Her entire identity had been torn to shreds.

"Let's go sit down," Link Parskey instructed, leading her up to a table at the front of the courtroom.

Charlotte sat, and stayed there while others began to filter into the room, filling the rows of pews at her back. She refused to look at them. She recognized some voices as belonging to important television people and even a few coworkers, and didn't recognize others; she refused to look all the same, not wanting for any of this to be real. It all seemed like a terrible dream. She needed to maintain that numbness, a sense of detachment from herself.

The judge walked in and took up his seat, and so too did the jury file in shortly after. Everyone who needed to be there was in attendance, except for the plaintiff and his lawyers.

The judge cast his cool gaze across the room, the touch of his eyes like a winter wind. "Where is he?"

Charlotte noted that even the judge, a powerful man himself, refused to use Mamba's name, as if speaking of him was some sort of curse or hex.

Link Parskey leaned over and murmured in Charlotte's ear. "Don't get your hopes up."

She looked back at him, eyes wide, silently pleading. If Mamba didn't show up, he forfeited the trial.

The resounding echo of an opening door brought her spinning around, turning to look at the entrance to the courtroom. The crowd moved with her, dozens of heads craning to get a glimpse of the intruder.

A man strode in, a proud and tall man with a black suit tailored to fit his body like a set of scales. His hair was black as coal and his eyes–Charlotte gasped at the sight of them–were cold and somehow alien, reptilian in their disinterest. His features were angular and sharp, and he walked like a man who knew the world would bend to make room for his presence.

"Mamba," she whispered.

Mamba turned his dark snake's eyes in her direction. His lips thinned. He moved around her with uncanny grace and took up a spot at the other table. Behind him, unnoticed by her until just then, came not one lawyer, or two, but six lawyers outfitted in matching grey suits.

"Thank you for gracing us with your presence," the judge said, speaking the typically sarcastic words with utter respect and reverence.

Mamba folded his hands in front of him. His tongue flicked out, moistening his lips. "We will begin now," he said, his voice a firm and accentless hiss.

The judge nodded. "Court is now in session," he called.

The proceedings began.

Mamba sat there at his table, motionless, eerie, like a god amongst men while his team of lawyers beat the absolute shit out of Parskey. He put up a good attempt, but Charlotte knew from the very moment she saw Mamba that they would lose.

Media coverage agreed with her assessment. Against all her better judgment, she sat in front of the TV that night, watching the news for some sign of herself. A series of typical, boring stories left her hoping that no one cared about her anymore, that maybe the stir she had caused was less important than shootings and politics.

And then, it happened. The female journalist sitting at her desk, Windy Smothers, looked down at the papers in front of her with a harsh frown. "Now onto a topic we've been covering since it began. Charlotte Aria, the famous video blogger behind Living, Loving, Lifestyling, known colloquially as Triple L. With a sizable following in the millions, Charlotte gained traction by being a positive role model to young women. All that changed when she suddenly revealed herself to be anti-woman, anti-feminist, and anti-freedom of choice."

I'm none of those things!

Windy continued, naturally oblivious to Charlotte's internal protests. "Charlotte condemned a strip club known as Club Lollipop, and in doing so put down women everywhere. In this day and age, sex work is a proud trade, a job taken by strong women who use their body, looks, and physical abilities however they want. These women work hard for their money, and Charlotte made herself an enemy of self-proclaimed sluts everywhere in a video less than five minutes long.

"Charlotte's first day in court was today and judging by the temper of the crowd, she has lost all her fans and gained herself nearly as many haters." Windy looked straight at the camera with a scowl that had Charlotte shrinking back in her seat. "Many think that this is the fate she deserves. Women are liberated. This modern world accepts them. Charlotte had plenty of chances to get with the times–and failed. We will, of course, continue covering this case as the trial proceeds."

Charlotte didn't watch the news again after that. She was so confused about how her attempt to stand up for women had turned against her.

Luckily, or perhaps unluckily, the trial only took another two days. Afterward, the jury convened and returned a mere five minutes later with their verdict.

The foreman announced, "We the jury find Charlotte Aria guilty of all charges put against her. In order to make up for her grievous crime against the plaintiff, she will have to pay a fine of 10 million dollars. This fine will be paid in a series of monthly installments over the next three years. So say we."

And the judge agreed, and the court adjourned.

Charlotte lowered her head to the table and wrapped her arms around herself, so defeated she couldn't even cry. 10 million dollars was nothing to a man like Mamba, but it was enough to ruin her in a very short time. He knew it. She could feel his eyes on her as she slumped in her chair, and she could sense his satisfaction.

She had bitten him, but she was just a little mouse, and now he had bitten back.

Chapter Seven

His slave

HER FIRST MONTHLY PAYMENT to Mamba slashed her savings account in half. Charlotte watched the money disappear into one of his many accounts, perhaps belonging to an overseas bank where the fees were lower and no one would ask questions. She wanted to weep at the partial destruction of what she'd worked to build for so long, but all she could do was sit there in a state of utter and absolute numbness.

She'd had that account since before she was born, when her parents opened it up in her soon-to-be-name to start funneling money in to provide for her future. As the years had passed and she got birthday money and worked summer jobs, she stowed nearly all of it away in that account. It became a mix between an emergency fund and a retirement fund. She took from it only sparingly, to buy her first car, to pay for college. When her career took off, she stopped digging into her savings. Stopped needing to. Since then, it had grown exponentially thanks to a dividend and her investments in stocks.

More than 32 years of money had been slumbering away, dormant, in that account, and now she was thrust back in time to when she was younger and still had financial troubles.

Charlotte nibbled her nails and rubbed her eyes with her hands, and sat back in her chair. "It's not so bad," she told herself, willing herself to believe it. She had her last paycheck coming and that would go directly into her checking account. She'd continue to get pay from the stocks she held, bulking up her savings again just in time to give her a comfortable buffer. The next month after that, she'd get more from her stocks and could do a third payment.

After that...

It was difficult to think about what could even possibly come after that. That was only three months and she had a total of 36 to get through. She'd be able to pull another month from her checking, but then she wouldn't be able to make the fifth. Maybe, if she combined the last of her savings and the rest of her checking...

It was going to be tight, she could tell, without even running the numbers. And what was she to do for the sixth month?

She had to count on getting a new job and very, very soon. And it had to be a good job. She couldn't flip burgers or hold a sign outside a car dealership.

Charlotte sat forward again and grabbed onto her computer and made a new email account, since Mamba hadn't relinquished her old one, or any of her social media, in the week since she lost the trial. She tapped out a series of quick emails to everyone whose addresses she could recall from memory, old friends and colleagues and connections who might be able to assist her. Some of the ones living in the city had to know of her recent disgrace and might be willing to help her in private. And those who were further away, she could get to them with her side of the story before the media had a chance to influence them.

It was a media circus everywhere she looked, so she had stopped looking. She was tired of hearing repeats of her supposed crime told in different words by various newscasters, and she was disgusted by the number of interviewees who were glad she'd lost the case.

Didn't they know she had been trying to help people like them?

Didn't they know the purpose of television was to entertain and that some details would be swept under the rug or glorified to make a better story?

Didn't they understand?

Or was all of this staged? A huge conspiracy?

Charlotte put her cheek on her hand and watched her computer screen, waiting for email responses from her contacts. As a content creator, she was naturally aware of all the weird corners of her platform where people rattled off about UFOs and how JFK's death could have been planned by the government. She'd disdained such content, which could corrupt the minds of younger viewers who didn't yet know how to separate fact from fiction. And now she was right in the middle of a conspiracy herself, or what sure as hell felt like one. Everyone could be bought for a certain price. Suppose Mamba had paid the television networks to portray her like this? He could easily select supporters of his or even actors that he wanted to appear on TV with pre-chosen opinions.

If only she was in a movie. Right about now, she'd be finding a key piece of information to confirm her suspicions. Like the underdog she was, she'd come out on top and take down Mamba, and cause his entire scheme to unravel.

Unfortunately, it wasn't a movie.

She held out hope, but it didn't last very long.

Practically no one replied to her emails. One of the few responses came from someone she didn't know, as she'd messed up one of the addresses and accidentally sent it to them. The recipient told her this, then professed their undying hatred for her.

The other people who replied, former friends, colleagues, expressed a mix of sympathy and disdain, though all made it clear they wanted nothing to do with her for their own safety.

Forced to start anew, she put out resumes, sending them to large companies where her particular skills could be of use.

All responses came back negative, and that was if she was given a response at all.

Another month passed, and then two. She was able to pay her installments exactly as she had predicted, though now the situation was dire. Worse still, she had run out of respectable companies to apply to. She'd been contacting potential employers as far away as a two-hour drive and still no one even wanted to give her an interview.

She was absolutely, utterly alone.

Her appetite decreased and she stopped eating more than once a day, if that. She tried to be cheerful about it and would tell herself she was losing weight, with the added bonus that her food would last longer and she'd have to pay less. Cheer wasn't a thing that came easy and soon she stopped pretending.

Around that time, she stopped going outside.

The media attention around her had died down, having done all the damage they could. People saw her and knew who she was. They spat on her, tripped her when she walked, pushed and shoved her. They threw insults at her from across the other side of the road, sometimes even risking getting run over to come over and deliver their taunts face-to-face. And sometimes, a reporter, always looking bored, always clearly having drawn the short straw, would be lingering right outside the building to catch her.

Best to stay inside.

Best to bunker down and bear this siege as best she could, though her walls were cracking and crumbling all around her.

The fourth month came and went, leaving her with so little that paying the rent on her apartment almost broke her spirit for good.

The fifth month did break her, the final straw on her back. No, the final boulder on top of the avalanche on her back. She couldn't make it, even when pooling the last scraps of her money together. Even selling her stocks was a mere drop in the bucket.

Deadline looming, she knew she had no choice.

Charlotte drank an ungodly amount of coffee, pacing in a jittery fashion in her apartment until night fell over the city. She waited another two hours after that, wearing a path on her carpet, and then she made her move.

Under the cover of night, with big sunglasses obscuring most of her face, she drove to a pawn shop that looked at least halfway respectable. Stepping out of the car into the cool of near-winter, frost shimmering on her breath, she took a shoebox from her passenger seat. She tucked the shoebox under her arm and hustled through the chill and through the door, beside which flashed a dull "open" sign.

The air in the shop was thick with the odor of cigar smoke and desperation. A man, smoking a fat cigar, turned his ruddy face in her direction. "Out late."

It wasn't a question. Charlotte hurried up to him with her shoebox and set it on the counter in front of him. As the only customer, she felt she had a right to get down to business before he invited her to. "How much can I get for all of this?" she demanded, and took the lid off the box.

A tangle of jewelry gleamed in the harsh bare bulbs dangling over the counter, coils of silver chain and gold bangles, amethyst earrings, diamond necklaces, all of it very tasteful and classy and yet so gaudy when jumbled together in such a manner.

The man pinched out his cigar and set it aside on an ashtray, which already seemed to bear the remnants of several other rolls. He reached for the box and pulled it closer to him. His fingernails were yellow from tobacco. "Can I?"

She wanted to say no. She nodded. "Go ahead."

He tipped over the shoebox and let all her jewelry spill out onto the glass top of the counter. He ran his fingers through the shining mess, sifting it around to look at the contents. "Why are you wanting to pawn all this?" he asked. In little deft movements that surprised her, he sorted earrings and rings and bracelets and necklaces all into separate piles.

"I'm having money troubles. I need cash, and I need it now."

"Bank loan," he suggested. He picked up two tangled necklaces and swiftly parted them despite the size of his fingers in comparison to the fine links.

"Not fast enough. I can't wait for approval."

"Lady, no such thing as fast money unless you screw for it."

A chill ran down her spine. She'd sell her furniture, her fridge, her microwave. She'd set up a lemonade stand. Anything but prostitution. Anything but that. Her body was all she had left. If she gave up that, if she defiled her own sanctity, there was no point for her to have done this in the first place.

"There's at least $100,000 worth here." He looked up at her. "Anything over 10k needs to go through the boss and he ain't going to be here until tomorrow."

Her heart dropped. She put her hand on the counter to steady herself. The glass was hot under her fingers. "Are you kidding? This is worth at least five times that!"

"Maybe when you bought it new from the store with the brand name right on the box and label. Now it's used. And we'll have to authenticate every piece to make sure it's legit. That costs us time and money. And no customers come in looking for pieces like this on the regular. Depends on what the boss says tomorrow, but it won't be much more than that." The man shrugged. "Fast cash ain't much cash. Now you know."

Now she knows.

She returned the next day and spoke with the owner of the store, who took her back to his office and evaluated each piece in a process that lasted for a full hour. He also looked like a smoker and had greasy hair, but he was professional and spoke honestly. He gave her the price for each individual piece–what he was willing to pay–and then gave her the total at the end.

Charlotte tried to get a bit more out of him, telling him having such nice jewelry would increase his notoriety, but he refused.

She accepted, and made her fifth payment just in time.

And then she was out of money. The bank wouldn't give her a loan, citing reasonable concerns. She went away convinced they didn't want to be associated with her.

That left her with a final course of action. She made an appointment with the judge who had overseen her case and appealed directly to him while he sat in his chair at the front of the courtroom between trials. She asked for an extension, a retrial. Anything.

He looked down at her while she pleaded, and then at his watch. The second hand ticked ticked ticked, made a half rotation before he deigned to speak.

"I'm sorry, but the matter is beyond me now. A ruling was reached. I can't just change it. It's illegal and it would also be a terrible precedent to set for other criminals."

Other criminals. I'm not a criminal.

"What am I supposed to do?" she asked, her voice echoing across the high ceiling.

The judge shrugged at her. "Ask for a retrial. Or speak to the plaintiff directly. He's the one who has the power to help you now."

"He's the one who ruined me in the first place!" she cried, on the very verge of panic. The details of the contract she'd signed with Mamba made it very clear failure to pay would result in jail, and that each subsequent missed payment would mean more jail time.

Basically, if she went to jail, she would be staying in jail. Lacking a way to make money, she'd go right back in as soon as she got out.

The judge looked at her with eyes so cold, though not as cold as Mamba's. "You are the one who tried to ruin him. He just did it better than you. Our time is up, Miss Aria."

Charlotte turned away from him and walked down the aisle in the middle of the room, struggling to breathe through her dismay.

Could she do it, talk to Mamba?

Did she dare?

Chapter Eight

On your knees

I can't believe I'm doing this. I can't believe I have to do this.

Charlotte swallowed what remained of her protestations and called Champion Media's head office, using a burner phone she'd bought for a piddly sum of money some years ago. Ever a sensible woman, she had an emergency kit she could grab out of her closet whenever she needed to run, in the case of some sort of attack or natural disaster. The kit contained a supply of nonperishable food, clothes, toiletries, money, and this phone, in case there was no time to get her real one. She'd already used the money and the toiletries to keep from having to spend more.

The burner phone was a pay-as-you-go sort. She hoped the call would be brief and the cost minimal.

After a few seconds of staticky ringing, there was a click and a woman's voice echoed through the terrible connection. "Champion Media, head office, Princess Harlemaine speaking. How can I help you to-day?"

Charlotte winced as the woman's falsetto grated on her ear. Her voice was as fake as her name, a singsong probably forced upon her by Mamba.

Get it together. Talk!

"Hello, my name is Cha..."

"You have been asked not to contact anyone in this company," the secretary interrupted her, her warbling voice now mocking. "Please hang up now or I will be forced to report you to the police for harassment."

"I need to speak with Mamba!" she yelped, digging her toes against the carpet. "Please. I wouldn't if I didn't have to. Please just forward me to him, or give me his number. Something. Anything."

"Please hang up now or I will be forced to report you."

Charlotte pushed her fingers to her eyes, panting, her pulse thrumming in her ears.

Someone murmured something on the other end of the line, out of earshot. Princess responded, her high voice dulled to a squeak now. She must have had her hand over the speaker.

"Are you still there?" Princess the secretary asked, voice clearer now.

"Yes. Please..."

"Luckily for you, I was just given permission to transfer you. Please hold while I do so."

Princess's voice was replaced by scratchy jazz tunes, trumpets bleating and piano notes fluttering in and out. It was a step up from elevator music and did nothing to calm Charlotte's nerves.

The music stopped almost as soon as it had come, a trumpet dying mid-wail.

"Mamba speaking." He sounded exactly the same as he had nearly six months ago. His voice was a measured and smooth hiss, lacking any true identifying characteristics. Had she not seen him and known what he looked like, she wouldn't have been able to identify him. He could have been anyone, from anywhere, skulking just out of sight in a dark corner.

"Who is this?" he continued.

Somehow, she found her voice. "Charlotte Aria."

"No. Your name means nothing to me," Mamba said smoothly, darkly. "Tell me who you are."

"I-I'm the woman who lost the defamation suit against you."

"Yes, I recall now," he purred.

You recall? You recall? Charlotte wanted to tear her hair out. This bastard. She meant so absolute little to him that he'd forgotten her existence.

No. He was messing with her. He had to be.

"What is it you want? I am a very busy man with no time for riffraff such as yourself."

Riffraff. Such a silly insult, almost outdated, and yet it tore deep.

"I need to see you," Charlotte said. "Urgently."

"Then you can schedule an appointment, though you can expect a considerable wait time as I am a man very much in demand."

A wait time of a week, a month? A year?

"Please," she said. "It has to do with the contract I signed with you."

His voice went sharp, cold, like a knife. "You aren't thinking of breaking it, are you? The repercussions would be fearsome."

"That's what I need to talk with you about! Please, please. Just five minutes. Two minutes!"

"Do you think I'm so fast as that? I assure you I tend to all my... dealings... with finesse and attention, and that takes time which I can't afford to waste on you."

"Please," she whispered. She slid off her chair and onto the floor, kneeling at the feet of the man on the other end of the phone. "I'm begging you."

Begging, like Katerina had begged for more when Charlotte was holding the remote to her vibrator. She felt sick, her stomach tingling. Other parts of her tingling too, in an inexplicable turn of events. She had never submitted to a man before like this and it was getting to her, and it was horrifying, mortifying. Her only comfort was that he couldn't see her.

"Beg," Mamba said flatly. "Beg me, Charlotte."

Her sinuses burned as tears stung her eyes, threatened to escape. Lowering her head, she pressed her lips close to the phone and choked out, "I'm begging you to let me come and see you. I'll come straight to you. I'll wait hours outside your office. I'll do anything. I just need to speak with you today. I know I have no right to ask that, but I am *begging...*"

Mamba spoke over her. "You will arrive at the door to my office in two hours and knock, exactly as the minute turns. You will enter when I call you in. We will discuss then. If you are even a second late, you will have missed your chance."

She nodded, even though he couldn't see her.

"Two hours," he repeated, and hung up on her.

Charlotte let her phone drop to the floor and hugged her arms around herself, trying to pull herself together. Her breasts felt sensitive and hot as her arms slid over herself. Her nipples protruded, twin turgid peaks beneath her bra and shirt.

Guilt stole through her at her arousal. Begging like that was so shameful and to be turned on like that from it made her a traitor to her own beliefs. The more she thought about it, the hornier she got, the harder her pussy pounded for attention.

It's only hormones. Adrenaline. My body reacting to increased blood flow. I don't have to have enjoyed what just happened for me to be feeling this way.

She did have two hours to spare...

Charlotte got to her feet and padded out of her home office to her bedroom. She went to her dresser and opened the underwear drawer and pushed all her modest panties aside to reveal a slender pink cylinder. She lifted the dildo out and took it over to the bed with her, and held it in her lap while sitting on the edge of the mattress. She had chosen this one many years ago because it was smooth and didn't look anything at all like an actual dick, having only a few ridges and a bulb on the one end for added enjoyment. It hardly got any use these days.

Everything else in her life had changed, so why not this?

Charlotte lay back on her bed and lifted up her hips to slide down her pants and panties. Her pussy was hit with a cold draft when exposed, causing her muscles to contract and her labia to curl inward. The tension felt good and she kept her muscles tightened, squeezing her inner walls, while pulling a blanket over her lower body to keep the cold out. She didn't want to watch, anyway. When encouraging young girls to explore themselves, using delicate language, Charlotte encouraged them to get familiar with what they looked like down there. Use a mirror. But she had seen it all and found it boring and not particularly pleasing to see.

Charlotte spread her legs and ran the rounded tip of her dildo down her inner thigh to her clit, caressing the sensitive nub of flesh. She worked her dildo in circles around her clit, pressing on it from all angles. Every press sent a nice wave of heat to her core. She felt herself starting to get wet, her body preparing to be entered. She held off, knowing herself well enough to recognize that she wasn't quite there yet.

Instead, she positioned the length of the dildo against her clit and started rubbing in strokes that ran parallel to her slit. She angled her wrist so the dildo's girth also glided between her lips, creating a terrific back-and-forth of friction that had her hips starting to wiggle along.

A moan rose up the back of her throat. She restricted it, thinking such guttural sounds to be unattractive.

After a certain point, the rubbing stopped doing much for her and seemed boring. She could rub and rub all day, she felt, and never get anywhere, which was strange because this was often all she needed.

I wanted this, didn't I?

She thought back, through the haze of sexual desire clouding her mind, to what had aroused her in the first place.

Begging Mamba to let her come and see him.

"Please," she whispered aloud, to see how it felt. She closed her eyes and imagined his flat stare pinning her from above.

That strange and mortifying tingle from before swept through her, causing her pussy to spasm. She gasped, couldn't help it, and spoke another, more breathless plea to the apparition of Mamba in her mind. Her hand seemed to have a mind of its own, angling the dildo towards her pussy entrance. She thrust the rounded end inside herself and bucked on it, taking it in her, shoving it deeper each time until the heel of her hand struck her clit with each push. Her body exploded. She gritted her teeth around a yell. A newer, hotter wetness coated her pussy lips, wet her fingers as she continued thrusting.

Finally, the tremors stopped and she pulled the dildo from her tremulous interior. When it was out of her, the realization of what she had done hit her. The guilt from before returned and she cringed, curling up on her side. She hid her face, but she couldn't hide from herself. She couldn't lie to herself.

Being disgraced had turned her on. She could say it was hormones and such all she liked, but she'd only been able to orgasm when she returned to the subject. That said something about her and she didn't like it, not at all.

Tears trickled down her face. Charlotte rolled over onto her stomach and pulled a pillow over, and cried against it as the shame wracked through her. She was becoming someone unrecognizable. She hadn't done anything to deserve it.

When at last the tears had run their course, she felt empty, drained. Or maybe that was her recent orgasm. Either way, she felt worse rather than better and so regretted what she had done.

She wasn't done yet with those regrets, either. She still had to go see him and talk to him in person.

Sniffling a bit, she sat up. She swung her legs out of bed and bent to pick her clothes up off the floor. She sighed out, breathed in, and smelled the muskiness of her recent sex in the air, faint but present, like a secret no one wanted to discuss.

If she went to see Mamba while smelling of sex, well, that would be the most awful thing imaginable. That would be like shooting herself and then jumping into an ocean. She'd attract sharks.

She'd attract *him*.

A look at her clock confirmed for her that she would have enough time to shower before she had to get on the road. She shed the rest of her clothes on the way and hopped in. She took no pleasure in the hot water trailing down her skin, the soft suds of soap perfuming the air with the sweet scent of lavender. It was all business, all purpose.

Climbing out, she dried off and focused on putting herself back together. Her eyes and nose were red from crying. She covered it up with concealer and foundation, and applied a bit too much lipstick until she looked like a teenage girl just beginning to play with makeup. By that point, she didn't have the time or patience to fix it, so she added eyeshadow to match. She also spritzed herself with some perfume, and then a little more, enough to make the entire bathroom smell like a floral arrangement on a hot summer day. Even then, she thought she could still detect the smell of sex around her. It surrounded her like an aura.

There wasn't any time to do anything else. She grabbed her car keys and her burner phone and left her apartment to go haggle for her life.

Chapter Nine

Entertain me

CHARLOTTE HAD NEVER BEEN to the very top floor of CM, had never had reason to. All her dealings had gone through Damian. He represented a sort of ceiling, since she'd never had reason to go above him. Now she had ascended him, past the attic, into a spiraling tower that went up and up. What she would find at the very top, she didn't know, but she had a suspicion she wouldn't like it at all.

Once she stepped out of the elevator, she found herself in a spacious waiting area. The floor shone like a polished mirror. She could see her reflection. A glance down between her feet confirmed that she didn't actually want to. A slight warping of the light turned her purple-lip-sticked mouth into a garish, clownish slash.

A huge flat white desk took up an entire corner of the lobby and behind that desk sat a bespectacled secretary. She was the secretary Charlotte had spoken to on the phone. She had no doubt about that. This was a woman who would absolutely call herself Princess, who would throw the pitch of her voice up an octave to be pleasing to pen. Her hair was silky and brown with blonde highlights, parted and swept over to one side. A black-and-white crop top strained to contain her breasts, leaving her smooth, tanned stomach exposed. That was all Charlotte could see of her with the desk in the way and it was more than she had wanted to.

Princess shifted her glasses to peer over the tops of them and narrowed her eyes. "He'll be with you in a minute. Take a seat."

When she shifted her glasses, the light reflecting upon them didn't warp, as they would have if the lenses were a prescription. They were fake, part of her sexy secretary costume.

"Thank you," Charlotte said, her mouth dry. She crossed the floor, her heels tapping a staccato beat, and sat down on the couch. It was a long winding stretch of cushion that ran the length of the wall, with ottomans placed near each concave curve. Plush pillows lined the couch back. She couldn't relax, refused to relax, and kept her spine stiff and straight.

Expensive pieces of abstract art covered the other walls, even high up above a window showing an impressive view of the city below. Charlotte found herself particularly attracted to a square painting, mostly gray in coloration, with swipes of blue above and green below. Twists of darker and lighter gray and splashes of red brought to her mind some sort of battle, perhaps Medieval.

She wondered how much it had cost. She wondered if this was what the top floor always looked like, or if Mamba had changed it to suit his needs.

How much has he changed? Was I just the first adjustment he made?

Princess spoke, butting into her thoughts. "He's ready for you now."

Charlotte got up and went to the door, all that separated her from the man trying to ruin her life. Recalling the instructions she had been given, she watched the clock on the wall and timed her knock with the first tick of the new minute.

"Enter," his voice called. When raised, it had a rough undertone.

Knowing she had no hope of preparing herself, Charlotte shoved his door open and thrust herself into his office.

The room unfurled around her, cavernous in size, lined with gigantic photographs and paintings of scantily-clad women in all sorts of scandalous positions. Backs were arched unnaturally, thrusting out their breasts and asses, which were all too large and perfectly round to be natural. Platinum-blonde hair, always platinum-blonde, spilled over their shoulders, down their backs, trailed over their rotund asses. Their lips were plump, unnaturally so, and shiny with makeup. Their faces were blank, lustful, high color in their cheeks as they arched and stared upwards.

Even in the paintings, those details were clear. The artists had rendered their models with hyper-realistic details,

Charlotte stood there, framed on all sides by the pornographic images. They showed her what this man was really like, what he really wanted of his women, as if she'd had any doubt. He saw all women as the same, all women as whores. She was another whore to him, too. A money whore, come to try and suck him dry.

Mamba sat far across at the other end of the room, in front of an entire wall of window panes, showing the city below. Shorter skyscrapers, office buildings, clusters of stores, strip malls, and the roads that wove through it all, covered in cars and rimmed with pedestrians; he lorded over it all like a king at his throne. He even wore the modern man's equivalent of king's clothing, an expensive suit tailored to fit his tall, muscular body.

"So you're smart enough to listen to instructions," he said, and gave a dry smirk that chilled her to the bone.

Charlotte clasped her hands in front of her and held her head high, trying not to show him that she was intimidated. She took a step forward.

"Don't come closer," Mamba said. His voice was still so smooth and measured and he still smiled, but it was an obvious command.

Charlotte froze where she stood, heart thundering in her breast. As much as she didn't want to, she had to obey him. Her future depended upon it.

Mamba folded his hands on his executive desk, smiling that unpleasant smile. "You aren't fit to approach me. Tell me what it is you want and be quick about it. While I'm wasting time with you, I fall behind on more important matters."

This is the most *important matter to* me, she thought. He had no sympathy for her. She hadn't expected him to and it was still disheartening to see for herself.

"Speak," he commanded.

She recalled how he had wanted her to beg before. It might well be her only chance to appeal to his ego. She forced herself to lower her head and spoke while looking at the gleaming white expanse of floor. Her voice echoed across the vastness of the room.

"Mamba, I can't afford to keep paying you. I've done everything I can, but I'm absolutely broke. There's no more money left in my bank accounts. I've sold all my jewelry to reach last month's payment. Now there's nothing left. Please. I'm begging you. Can we come to some sort of agreement? You won't get any money at all if I go to jail for defaulting on the payments. Only you can help me."

Mamba suddenly started laughing as she finished. His shoulders quivered with an evil merriment at her expense. His laughter cut off quickly and he leaned forward in his chair, glaring at her with his cold venomous eyes. "I'm sure you've noticed that hardly anyone dares speak my name. They seem to think talking of me will summon me."

That's how this happened to me, she thought bitterly. She said his name too many times and he came at the summons, like a ghoul, a demon, rising out of darkness to ruin her.

"From now on, you will address me as sir."

He didn't elaborate on what would happen if she didn't. He didn't need to. The implications were clear.

Charlotte lowered her head. "Yes, sir."

"Why should I prevent your life from being ruined when you attempted to do the same to me?" Mamba asked. "You tried to play a game in which you didn't know the rules. You brought this upon yourself. You played with fire. Whether you burn yourself is none of my concern. Do you understand? I don't care about you. Not at all. You're nothing. A worm. An ant. An annoying speck of dust."

Tears stung her eyes. "Then why," she whispered, voice trembling, "are you doing this? If you really don't care?"

"That's business." He lifted one shoulder in a careless shrug. "You are a demonstration of what happens when people try to mess with me. You're a tool. Unfortunately, you are a very old and outdated tool capable of only one thing. I can use you, but only this once. You aren't a real woman. You can do nothing more than this and soon your time will be finished. You'll be broken. And then you will go to jail with the other pieces of garbage."

Charlotte came to a realization while Mamba spoke. It was that one sentence in the middle that gave her true insight into the deeper meaning of what he was saying. She wasn't a "real woman" in his eyes. The fake whores, more plastic than person, lining his walls were what he considered to be real women. He wanted tools. He wanted big-lipped and busty females who would perform whatever task he wanted and fill every role he required of them.

Despite all his claims to support the empowerment of women, he had just revealed himself to her as a complete and utter misogynist.

If only she'd been wearing a microphone or had a recorder in her pocket, she could have recorded him and fought back.

Maybe he's right. I'm old. I don't know what I'm doing anymore. Maybe this is what I deserve.

She risked a glance up at Mamba and saw him grinning, gloating, more than likely able to read every thought that crossed her face. This was what he wanted, for her to give up, for her to believe what he said about her.

The urge swept through her to show him her middle finger and storm out. Fuck him. Fuck everything he stood for. She'd find a different, less degrading way to get through this.

"What are you considering?" Mamba's eyes narrowed to slits. He thrummed his fingers on his desk, the tapping echoing like gunshots in the cavernous office. "You want to pretend to be a bad bitch and storm out of here. How very noble of you to stick to your guns even in what is so clearly a desperate time for you. You'd have my admiration, except I can reassure you that you won't make it very far and you will get very little done. You've learned nothing from this whole ordeal."

"What am I supposed to learn? Sir," she added, lamely.

"That you are no better than any other woman. You are no different, though you think you are and so you have pigeonholed yourself. But you are not different. You think I can't tell you orgasmed recently?"

She couldn't have been more shocked than if he'd thrown a bucket of ice water in her face. She sputtered, "What... How..." She shifted her clasped hands, subconsciously covering her pussy. She'd showered. She'd put on perfume. He shouldn't know that she'd had an orgasm. It had to be a trick.

The confidence in his smirk told her that no, it wasn't a trick. He really knew. He could really tell. She may as well have been naked and standing in front of him with her pussy wet for all she could hide from him.

"I will write off one month's payment," Mamba said in his slow hiss. "This month. You'd best do all you can to get back on your feet in that time."

She was too relieved to argue with him about how he'd ruined her reputation so thoroughly she might as well not have feet to stand on. He'd chopped them off, amputated her foundation.

"In return, you will dye your hair my favorite color."

His favorite color. Blue, like the sadness he inflicted upon others? Or red, like the blood of his enemies?

She was about to ask when it hit her. "No," she breathed.

"Yes. Platinum-blonde. You will do it and you will send me proof. No sooner and no later than I receive your proof, I will write off the payment you owe this month."

The same color as the girls in Club Lollipop. The same color as all these women rimming his office. Whore hair. Stripper hair.

Anger rose in her throat. "You can't be serious."

"You're angry. That's very funny to me, that you still have the audacity to be mad after all this." Mamba laughed aloud. "You must know that dying your hair will cost far less than what you owe me for this month. Even if you went to the best stylist in town."

He stopped laughing rather abruptly and leaned back in his chair, as if bored with her. "That is my offer. Take it or leave it. I, of course, don't need the money you owe me, but you do need this break. Are you going to be such an uppity bitch that you won't do it? Then go to jail. That would amuse me, to see you behind bars. I might have to visit you and see how you're faring. You will have to introduce me to whatever butch woman decides to use you as her bitch."

She absolutely couldn't believe this. But hadn't she said she'd do any-thing? This was her only way out. Damn the insufferable man for making sense. Damn him.

"Get out of my office." Mamba swiveled in his chair, ignoring her, gazing out at his view of the city.

"Yes, sir," Charlotte murmured. She turned and got out of there as fast as her legs could carry her.

Chapter Ten

Gush

"ARE YOU SURE YOU want to do this?" the hairstylist asked, holding strands of Charlotte's dark coffee hair in either hand. "Your hair is so beautiful. It compliments your skin and your eyes so nicely."

Charlotte stared at herself in the huge mirror, hardly able to recognize the woman reflected back. She had lost weight and her face was thinner, making her eyes look bigger–though the bags underneath them kept her new skinniness from being attractive.

No, she didn't want to do this, but she had no choice in the matter.

"I'm sure," she lied.

The stylist, Wendy, a nice and matronly woman with huge breasts and an equally large bottom, lifted her heavy shoulders in a shrug. "It's your money and your time, honey. You know this will damage your hair no matter how carefully we do this."

Maybe it will all fall off.

"I trust you. I'm safe in your skilled hands," Charlotte deadpanned.

Wendy gave another shrug. "Well, okay. Let me go ahead and get the first round of bleach ready."

"I can't wait."

Wendy seemed not to pick up on the sarcasm and smiled before wandering away, disappearing into a sort of supply area in the back. Laughter came from the room as she talked with another stylist, though their voices were too indistinct for Charlotte to eavesdrop on the conversation.

Charlotte tapped her fingers on the arm of her chair and looked around the beauty parlor. She visited a similar place every couple of months to get her hair trimmed and her hands softened with a wax treatment. She never spent more than an hour in the place, and therefore didn't really know anyone there beyond a few names and the occasional face. That suited her fine, since she didn't believe in vanity. Simply taking care of one's appearance wasn't the same.

Now she was here for the sake of someone else's vanity and that felt twice as wrong.

She had come early in the morning, as soon as the place opened, though she wound up waiting half an hour for Wendy to arrive, since none of the other girls wanted to risk doing her hair themselves. There was only one other person in the shop, an elderly woman with hair that specific shade of orange that had never been naturally found on a human head. She was chattering away to her stylist while getting her hair shampooed, curls and ripples of foam building over her dyed locks.

"Here we are," Wendy announced, approaching with a bowl in her hands. The harsh chemical scent of bleach flooded Charlotte's nose. She tried not to gag and switched to breathing through her mouth.

Wendy set the bowl down and grabbed a cape to wrap around Charlotte's neck, "So," she said, "Charlotte, what made you want to go for such a drastic color change?"

Charlotte almost gagged again, though it was from the question this time and not the foul stench of bleach. She very well couldn't tell this woman the truth, which meant she was going to have to lie.

"I just thought it was time for a change," Charlotte responded. Wendy began to paint her head with the cold bleach, one layer of hair at a time.

"Platinum blonde is a very exciting color," Wendy responded, her voice a soft hum as she worked. "And growing very popular. Even for men."

I should have told Mamba to dye his hair. It would have been worth it.

He would never alter his appearance in a million years, especially not at the request of a lowly female. That was the woman's job, to conform to his desires.

"What made you want to come to us?" Wendy asked, doing what hairstylists did best: chatter. "I always like to know what brings new customers in."

"I didn't want anyone at my usual salon to see me," Charlotte replied. The truth, though Wendy wouldn't pick up on the severity of it. "I don't think I'd have been able to get it done there. They'd have kept trying to convince me otherwise."

SHAMEFUL ADDICTIONS   99

Wendy chuckled, and rotated Charlotte a bit on the turning chair. She dabbed her brush in her paint, slathered Charlotte's hair, and dabbed in again, swirling around the perimeter of the bowl. "Well, I also tried to convince you otherwise. A lot of stylists get told that certain things can't be done. The truth is they usually can be, but it takes a lot of time and an experienced hand. I've been cutting hair for twenty years now. More than that, if you count childhood experiments on my toys using craft scissors."

Charlotte smiled a little, despite the awful situation. She really did like Wendy on principal. The older woman had a completely natural body and hadn't slapped a ton of makeup on her face, and she was dressed in comfortable and casual clothes. If not for the reason Charlotte was getting her hair dyed, she might have settled in and actually enjoyed herself.

The first round of bleach went on. Wendy gathered up Charlotte's gooey hair under a plastic cap and put her aside to let the chemicals do their thing. Half an hour later, Wendy checked on her.

"Yep," Wendy said, peeking under the cap. "Exactly what I thought."

"Is it... orange?"

Wendy chuckled and shook her head. "No. But it's hardly lightened at all. Unfortunately, I can't just let you sit around with bleach on your head or things really will go badly."

Charlotte swallowed hard. "So now what?"

Wendy led her back to the chair in the main salon. "Now we rinse it out and do it again. And again. And again. Until we get the right color. That's what's going to take so long, hon. Beauty takes time."

Charlotte looked at herself, her thin face and looser shirt and her hair all piled up on top of her head. Was this beauty? She didn't think even Mamba would agree.

Wendy leaned her back in the chair and turned the water on. She splashed a little bit on Charlotte's head. "Too hot?"

"No, it's fine."

"Do you want your eyebrows lightened, too? We can do that much quicker near the end."

"Why not," Charlotte said. She'd already sunk this far into depravity, she might as well keep going.

Wendy finished rinsing out Charlotte's hair and then conditioned it. "To help it stay healthy," she said.

With her hair washed, Wendy then set about to slowly and thoroughly drying it, both to minimize damage and because wet hair made the bleaching process unpredictable.

"Do you want to take a peek? See if you like this shade and want to stop?"

Charlotte laughed, without humor. "A last-ditch attempt to talk some sense into me?"

"Yes."

"I don't think so. I don't want to look until it's done."

"Don't want to spoil the surprise?" Wendy smiled.

Charlotte studied her hands. "Something like that."

If she looked, if she saw herself, she thought she might chicken out. She didn't want to see herself transform. She just wanted it to be over with so she could take a picture and send it to Mamba.

Another round of bleach went onto her hair, and then she was sent off to a back room again, where she held a magazine in her hands and pretended to care about the lives of celebrities.

More rinsing, more drying, more bleaching.

Hours of monotony.

Hours of her life, precious hours being wasted in the pursuit of a beauty standard she would never be able to comprehend.

Evening had arrived by the time Wendy finally washed and dried her hair for the last time. "Go ahead and take a look," she encouraged. "We're done."

Charlotte felt herself be turned to face the mirror. She opened her eyes, slowly, and looked at herself.

At the woman she was now.

Her thick, lovely dark hair was gone, replaced by that disgusting shade of white-blonde she disliked so much.

"What do you think?" Wendy gushed, sliding her fingers through Charlotte's hair. "It feels so different, too. Touch it!"

Charlotte lifted her hand, poked at her hair. It was so fine, almost brittle, she could hardly feel the strands on her skin. Even when she grabbed a handful and lifted it, she might as well have been holding air. She let the hair fall from her grasp and watched it cascade to lie limply over her shoulder.

"It's exactly what I wanted it to look like," Charlotte said, the only true compliment she could give the woman who had tried so hard for her. Tears stung her eyes. She forced them back.

Wendy beamed proudly and smiled so widely that Charlotte could see her molars. "That's always what I want to hear! Why don't you take a picture? Post it on your social media for all your admirers to gush over."

Charlotte winced, the unintentional jab striking her hard, going past her meager defenses. "I don't really have any social media."

"Well, you might want one to show your friends, still."

"Can you take it for me?"

"It would be my pleasure. I'd like to take one for myself, too, if you don't mind, to go along with what you looked like before?" Wendy pulled out her phone and held it up. "It would really amaze people if I post it on my website. I might get some new customers in."

Someone should be happy and fulfilled with their business life.

"I don't mind."

And then she would never ever be able to talk to Wendy again, because the pictures of her would bring in commenters to bash her. She had been lucky that Wendy didn't know who she was, but it wouldn't last. She wouldn't be getting another appointment with her. Hopefully, she wouldn't need to try to get one. Hopefully Mamba would be satisfied with the picture and be done with her.

Wendy took pictures with both phones, and then handed Charlotte's back to her.

"Thanks," Charlotte said. She stood up, scattering bits of her old, darker hair.

"You are so very welcome, Charlotte! Why don't we take this over to the counter?"

A sudden thought struck Charlotte while she was following the other woman over to her cash register. What if posting a picture of her online actually hurt Wendy instead of helping her? Suppose Wendy was then seen as a traitor to her sex as well?

Worse, she thought, handing the stylist her credit card, *what if people take this as a sign that I've changed my mind? What if they think I did this to try and get my support back?*

She could have moaned from despair. This wasn't going to end well at all, no matter the outcome. It was all terrible.

Charlotte finished paying the exuberant price and gave the stylist a massive tip. She walked out while Wendy was still stammering her thanks.

Back home, Charlotte sent the picture Wendy had taken to Mamba, through email. He responded almost right away, sending a message of approval and telling her that he would waive the month's payment. She would get a notification in the mail tomorrow.

Charlotte sighed and slumped back in her desk chair. It was over. It was done. She had some breathing room. How she was going to work up enough money in time for next month's payment was a mystery still, but she was certain she could find a way. Somehow.

Her computer screen went dark due to inactivity. Her reflection appeared, visible against the dark background. Her fine, pale new hair was shimmery and straight, framing her face in a way it hadn't before. Charlotte leaned forward, toying with it, bringing some of it forward to hang down against her cleavage. The stylist really had done a good job. It looked exactly like the hair of all the girls at Lollipop, and the kind the models had on the posters in Mamba's office. The silvery gloss of it was kind of nice against her soft, matte skin.

"What am I thinking?" she whispered. She shook her head and got up and left her office. She didn't look good at all. The hair didn't look good. It was whore's hair.

She would not fall victim to Mamba's mind control.

Chapter Eleven

Swallow it

The letter Mamba had promised arrived in the mail exactly when he had said it would, legal proof that she had no payment to make that month. Charlotte felt a huge weight lift from her shoulders and relief flooded through her. She sagged against the wall and let it carry her, bobbing along like a swimmer on her back in a calm river.

The relief didn't last long, thanks to a dam of doubt that sprang up ahead of her. This wasn't time to relax. She had to go out and do something about this, or else she'd find herself on the other side of that dam parched and on the verge of disgrace.

Charlotte pushed away from the wall and went into her bedroom to get dressed for the day, donning a simple purple dress and a pair of cheap earrings she hadn't been able to get rid of at the pawn shop. Force of habit saw her going into the bathroom to look at herself in the mirror.

But it wasn't her in the glass. It was that woman pretending to be Charlotte, wearing whore's hair.

Charlotte yanked her eyes away from the hair and looked at her outfit. Thanks to the weight she had lost, her clothes were growing too loose to fit properly. She was beginning to look like a true imposter. Like someone dressing up as someone they weren't. Maybe that wouldn't have been so bad if not for the looks she was getting. She looked homeless, like she had been forced to get the cheapest items available at a secondhand store.

There was another look besides the homeless one, and that one was even worse. Some of her loose clothes now hung just the right way to appear sluttery. Her too-big pants hung off her hips, flashing her panties–and even wearing a belt did nothing. Her shirts might slope off one or both shoulders, showing her bra, showing more of her breasts than she was comfortable with.

The dress she had chosen for the day was of the second variety. The dress could hang on one shoulder, or the other, not both at the same time. No matter which side she pushed the dress to, the angle revealed nearly the whole shape of her dress and plenty of cleavage beside.

She stared at herself in dismay. If not for the length of the dress, she could have been any run-of-the-mill whore about to work the street corners. This wasn't at all the image she wanted to convey, not for the place where she was going.

I need to change.

Charlotte left her bathroom and went to her dresser, but a glance at her phone stopped her. She was going to be late if she didn't get going right then. That wouldn't help her image at all.

She looked around in desperation and saw a jacket hanging on the back of her door. That would have to do. She pulled it on and shoved her feet into a pair of shoes and headed out.

A job fair was taking place downtown at a convention center. Many people from in and around the area were going to be there, searching for promising employees. Her hope was that, in such a public setting, her identity might go unnoticed. Then she could hand in her resume and maybe get a call or two. By that point, she'd have already won the potential employer over so that they might be willing to take a chance on her despite her reputation.

It was a long shot, but the fair was going to last all week, so she was getting a lot of chances there.

The center was packed, as she had hoped. Companies had set up booths all up and down the hallways, around which gathered crowds of hopeful people, all carrying copies of their own resumes and port-folios.

Charlotte pulled her jacket higher over her shoulders and ducked her head, and dove into the crowd.

Blend in, she told herself. *Blend in and it will all be okay.*

She cast glances out to either side, not wanting to show her face for too long at a time. She, and the others in the crowd in front of her, passed firms focused on data analysis, and companies wanting accountants and lawyers, and assistants, and secretaries. There was a veterinarian clinic, searching for lab techs, and a hospital looking to scope out a new round of nurses to take part in their programs. An architect was searching for an apprentice. A manufacturer of solar-powered devices was seeking help to fill out just about every department of his business.

Endless opportunities.

Charlotte made note of places where she could potentially be of assistance. While working as an assistant or secretary wouldn't net her nearly enough money to pay what she owed Mamba, perhaps having a job could help her convince him to work out a newer, better arrangement. It would show him that she was worth more than the sum of her parts.

A few hours passed while she walked and browsed, mapping out the place, reading up on the different companies and what they offered. One place needed a social media manager and she had plenty of experience in that department. Her hopes lifted.

"Hey, did you see that girl's hair?"

The whispered comment could have been about anyone. Charlotte knew that wasn't the case. Beyond a shadow of a doubt, someone was talking about her. She slowed, keeping her head low, letting her thin hair fall around her face to help disguise her.

"Wow," another voice murmured in response. "Pretty bold."

"Wait. Is she who I think she is?"

Charlotte stiffened. A trickle of sweat ran down her back.

"Charlotte Aria."

A gasp. "No fucking way. *She* got hair like that?"

Someone tapped Charlotte on the shoulder. Dread clawed at her insides. She turned. "Yes?" she asked, voice trembling.

Two girls stared at her, their eyes widening with judgment. The taller of the two exclaimed, "It really is you."

Now others in the crowd were turning, drawn in by curiosity.

"What the fuck are you doing here?" the tall girl demanded.

Charlotte opened her mouth to answer.

She wasn't given a chance.

"You think *you* deserve a job? What, it's been a few months and you think you'll be magically forgiven?" The girl jabbed her finger at Charlotte's chest. "Fuck off."

Charlotte pushed the girl's hand away. "Don't touch me."

"Don't touch *her!*" the shorter friend shrieked. "Bitch!"

Charlotte started backing away. She ran into someone and turned around, an apology already rising to her lips. Ten people stood behind her, forming a sort of ring at her back, with more behind them. "Excuse me." She stepped forward. Cruel hands pushed at her, shoved her back.

Angry shouts flew from the crowd, the fury of the original two girls spreading, worked into a frenzy by mob mentality. Charlotte flashed back to the horrendous scenes in and outside of the courthouse and felt dizzy.

A man in a black uniform shoved his way through the crowd, arms waving. "Back up!" he commanded. "Back up! What the hell is going on?"

The shorter girl pointed at Charlotte. "She pushed my friend!"

"What?" Charlotte exclaimed, forgetting herself in her outrage. She was meant to be the sympathetic figure here, the one people would want to empathize with and give a chance. But damn, all of this was so unfair. "I was minding my own business!"

The security guard threw a sharp glare at the crowd. "You're all making a scene. Get out of here. Leave this to the person whose *job* it is to handle this."

No one seemed interested in listening to him, though, not even with the veiled insult he threw at them. They only cared about Charlotte.

Charlotte spun, searching the crowd. Someone familiar stood against the far wall, as far away from her as they could possibly get. Link Parskey, now fully bald, his head gleaming under the light.

"Link!" Charlotte shouted, waving to him. "Link, please. You saw, didn't you?"

He defended me. He should have my back.

Link looked at her as though he had never seen her before in his entire life and walked away.

"No!" she cried, furious.

The security guard grabbed her by the shoulder. "Hey!" he barked, to get her attention. "Look, I know you're here to get a job, but you're causing a disturbance. Leave. Don't come back. Or I'll have to call the cops."

"Call the cops anyway," the taller girl shouted over his shoulder.

The guard rolled his eyes. "Just go, lady. I don't give a shit why these people hate you. But if you stick around, they'll tear you to pieces."

"But this is my chance!" Hot, flustered, Charlotte ripped her jacket off, which put her too-big dress–and her right breast–on full display. "I need this. Please. My resumes..."

"I'll call the cops," the guard sighed.

Horrified, Charlotte cried out again. "No!"

She was doing this to *avoid* going to jail!

She had no choice. Truly, she had no choice.

Charlotte backed away. Somehow, miraculously, the crowd parted around her to let her pass. She turned and made her way out of the convention center, pulling stares and glares after her the entire way. She was a magnet, pulling bad attention everywhere she went.

There was a trash bin outside the front door of the center. Charlotte tossed her resumes in there, to be with the other pieces of garbage.

She couldn't do that again.

She went back to applying for jobs online, to no avail. She applied for financial aid, and was denied.

She sold her car, and she broke her lease agreement to move to a smaller apartment. She auctioned off all but two pairs of her shoes, and even one night attempted to become a car-hire driver. The car-hire company turned her down, citing behavioral issues discovered during a background check.

At the end of that month, she was left in the same position where she had started.

Time to swallow her pride again.

She went to a salon an hour away to get her dark roots covered up and then went back to Mamba's office, showing up unannounced.

Princess, the secretary had been replaced by a near-identical clone by the name of Velvet.

Velvet motioned her to Mamba's door without so much as a greeting. Everyone knew why she was there, at that point.

She was getting numb to it.

Chapter Twelve

Cheeky dumb bitch

CHARLOTTE EDGED INTO THE room, which hadn't changed a bit since she had been there last. Neither had Mamba.

There did seem to be something *new* in the air she couldn't quite identify, a sort of heaviness or fullness. An atmosphere.

Mamba leaned back in his office chair and crossed his arms over his broad chest. "What do you want?"

Charlotte lowered her head. He might like that submissiveness and besides, it was easier to pretend she was submissive when she had done this once before already. "Sir, I'm back again because I can't afford to make the next payment."

Mamba grunted and shifted a bit in his seat, behavior which seemed odd coming from him. Charlotte didn't dwell on it. She didn't want to dwell on any of this. It was better to go along with whatever he wanted, whatever upsetting thing he required.

Mamba didn't say anything for a long moment, confusing Charlotte, because he had never been so delayed when responding before. He didn't seem to be thinking about anything. Rather, he looked a little blank, his eyes hazy.

In the silence, Charlotte thought she could hear something. It was difficult to pick up on, but there was a rhythmic sound in the room, quiet and fast and somehow odd. It reminded her almost of a machinery sound, a hum of electricity, the thrum of air-conditioning rattling through vents, yet was none of those. She would have described it as an organic sound, made by a living thing.

Mamba lifted his head and pinned Charlotte with an unnerving stare from his hazy black eyes. "Who are you?"

She stammered, caught off-guard. Maybe she didn't know what to expect from him after all. "I'm... It's Charlotte. Charlotte Aria?" Her voice rose from nervousness.

Mamba licked his lips and caressed his chin with his fingers, and tapped his cheek. "Charlotte, Charlotte. That name doesn't mean anything to me. Are you here to tryout for a spot at my new blowjob bar? Aria is a type of song. Will you make the men sing for you, Charlotte? Are you qualified to make them cum?"

Her mouth hung open. She realized how absurd she had to look, like she was begging him to stick something in there. She clenched her jaw and pressed her lips together.

Mamba chuckled. "I'll enjoy finding out. You'll have to wait your turn. I already have someone showing me their talents. You may be in luck, though. This one isn't doing a very good job."

The soft, steady, nearly inaudible sound increased in pace and grew somehow wetter.

Charlotte put her hand over her mouth as she realized what she was hearing, what was happening. Mamba's desk was so big. A woman could easily kneel under there and be *servicing* him. Trying out for a spot at his blowjob bar, whatever that was. The sound, it was sucking.

Someone under the desk was sucking Mamba's cock.

Mamba laughed again, and then he made another of those grunting sounds. She recognized it as pleasure, this time. "Of course I know who you are. What the fuck do you want?"

Charlotte smoothed her hands over her dress, the same purple one she had worn to her failed job fair outing. "I can't afford to pay you this month again," she whispered.

The sucking sounds paused.

Mamba pushed back in his chair a little and grabbed the hair of who-ever was under the desk. He clutched the long, platinum hair and gave a pull. "Harder," he commanded. "Faster."

The woman under the desk renewed her efforts. Charlotte could see her head bobbing up and down, her stomach flipping.

Mamba turned his attention to Charlotte again. "Are you a stupid cunt?"

He couldn't have surprised her more if he had gotten up and slapped her. "I-I don't know what you mean," she stammered. "I can't pay you this month."

Mamba narrowed his eyes and hissed from between his teeth, a sound that was part anger and part lust. "I asked you a question. Are you a stupid cunt? Is that why you can't figure this out? You get money. You pay me. That's the deal."

"I know." Heat rose to her face.

"Then are you a stupid cunt?" he repeated.

She refused to give him an answer.

She refused to be called names.

She was going to walk out of there and never come back.

If only. If only I could.

More heat flooded her face, turning her cheeks red as she accepted what she had to do. Charlotte closed her eyes and nodded. "Yes," she said, quietly.

"Yes, what?" Mamba drawled, his question turning into a moan from whatever the girl under the desk was doing to him. She was going at it harder than Charlotte knew was possible, rising all the way up, leaving his cock glistening and visible, before dropping back down and taking all of him into her mouth again. It looked so freeing.

Charlotte forced the words out of her mouth, to please him. "I'm a stupid cunt."

The relief of getting it over with, of having gotten through that disgrace, somehow managed to arouse her. She refused to believe it was from anything else except relief and an elevated heartbeat, that her nipples were stiffening against her bra. The hard peaks of her nipples rubbing over the fabric fed into her arousal, causing a warmth to pulse between her legs. It felt good, and it was so shameful all at once. He had to know, as well, that something was getting her off. He'd detected her orgasm somehow, despite her doing everything she could to hide it, even going so far as to shower to get rid of the musk of sex.

It clicked for her, that that was what hung in the air in the office. Sex.

"Good girl." Mamba's eyes went half-lidded. He repeated, "Good girl."

She didn't dare ask which girl in the room he referred to.

Mamba lowered his hands to his lap, gripping the hair of the girl sucking his cock. "You want me to write off another month."

"Yes. Please," she whispered, certain she had never been so humiliated in her entire life. She was being such a whore for him, begging for money, changing her hair color, submitting to his indomitable will.

"I told you before that you will call me Sir."

"Yes, Sir. Please, Sir." Her voice grew smaller and smaller with each word.

Mamba seemed to regain some of his true focus and sat up straighter in his chair, forcing the girl down beneath the desk again. He swung his head around to Charlotte. "As before, you will have to do something for me if you want me to write off the payment. It's a matter of principle that you must do something of worth in exchange. I am a man who follows through on my words because I know their value. You, on the other hand, need to be taught that you can't simply say whatever you want without a means by which to back them up."

Charlotte would have sworn she learned her lesson; he must want her to attend an entire course on the matter, which didn't give her much hope for the future.

"What do you want me to do this time?"

He wagged his finger at her, a mesmerizing gesture, like a cobra's sway just before it struck. "Will you do something for me in return?"

"What do you want?"

"Are you a cheeky dumb bitch, Charlotte?"

Charlotte lowered her head and bit her lip. The silence that passed between them was heavy, uncomfortable, interspersed with sucking sounds. "Yes," she whispered. "I'm a cheeky dumb bitch. Yes, I'll do something for you."

Mamba flashed a terrifying grin at her. He reached under the desk and pushed the girl away from him, then leaned forward in his chair. Charlotte was at an angle to see his lap, his huge wet cock, and her stomach knotted with warmth.

"Get a boob job," Mamba said.

She started, not sure if she had heard him right. "What?"

"Get. A. Boob. Job," he repeated, measuring out each word like he thought she was an idiot. Which, he probably did. And which she was. She was such an idiot for overstepping her bounds and getting herself into this terrible mess. "That's what you have to do. Take it or leave it, it makes no difference to me, though I'm sure it makes a hell of a lot of difference to you."

"But why?" she cried.

"Because," he growled, "I know we're going to be doing this for months. For years. You are never going to be able to get a job and you will never be able to make another payment for me."

She felt like she was falling, spiraling, his words pulling her into the abyss.

"We're going to be seeing each other for a very long time." He knitted his fingers together. "And I'm already tired of the way you look. You need improvement. Those tits of yours need help. Really, I'm doing you a favor here."

Charlotte put her hands over her breasts, felt their soft firmness. They weren't too big and they weren't too small. The perfect size, she had thought, enough to be womanly but not enough to be inconvenient. "But... they're already perky," she said, her voice faltering. She would have felt ridiculous if she wasn't so devastated.

"I've seen better," Mamba hissed. "And I never waste time on the imperfect. Either you get a boob job or I'm going to stop seeing you entirely. I'll get a restraining order against you, prevent you from even walking on the street in front of the building. Let's see you come in here and beg when you can't even come inside. What will you do, stand across the road and yell? Will you have a megahorn? Can you afford one, at this point?"

Charlotte clamped her hands over her ears. His mocking voice still penetrated, drilling into her.

"I'm losing patience with you, Charlotte. You're talking back to me. You have no right to do that."

Her chest heaved. Still with her hands over her ears, she whimpered, "I can't afford to get the surgery."

"I have a friend. I'll get you an appointment and pay for it out of my own money."

Alarm shot through her. "I'll be even more in debt to you!"

"You're right." He flashed that grin, his teeth like fangs. "It's only fair that you do something else for me right now to reimburse me for the cost."

"I don't want it!"

"I'm scheduling the appointment anyway. No matter what you do, it's going to be done. If you don't go, you don't get a pass for this month. If you don't do something for me right now, I'll have my friend charge you for his service. It's your choice."

None of this is my choice! she screamed internally. She didn't want any of this. It wasn't fair. This had to be illegal. But no one would listen to her if she came to them with a plea. Mamba was simply too powerful. He'd crush her every attempt, just like he had already done in the past.

"What do you want me to do?" The words came of their own will, belying her.

"I want you to show me your breasts." Mamba opened a desk drawer and pulled out a phone, a high-tech model that Charlotte didn't recognize. A prototype, or maybe the first of its kind, given to a powerful man as a favor before the product was announced to the public. "I want a 'before' picture so I can compare and admire the difference."

Charlotte turned, facing the exit to his office. The door was so near, so far away. The posters and paintings of sluts and whores around her watched her with judgmental eyes. She took a step towards the door, towards freedom, her mind racing. Other people stupider and less competent than her had found ways to avoid paying the price for their crimes. She could go on the run. She could cut her hair, shave it all off, dye it a new color, wear hoods to obscure her face from cameras and passersby who could be used to identify her. If she did that, her best bet was to flee the country, cross a border to make communicating more difficult for the police. Mexico was usually where fugitives from the law went, but she didn't see much point escaping if she was going to get herself killed soon after. If the gangs didn't, the bad water would.

Canada was a better option. Canadian hospitality. They were a sensible people, more like the kind of person she used to be before all this started. She could find shelter there, learn how to build an igloo, and ice fish for her meals.

And make friends with a fucking moose who will crush anyone who gets too close to me.

Her shoulders slumped as the already ridiculous fantasy took a turn towards the absurd and fantastical. People did run from the law all the time and sometimes they were even successful, but none of them had ever tried to escape from Mamba.

The man had erased her from existence, for fuck's sake. He would have no trouble at all finding her. He was that powerful. Godlike. And she was a plaything to be bent to his imagination.

Charlotte turned back to face Mamba, cheeks flushed, heart pounding. "Okay."

"Okay, what?"

"Okay, Sir." She tried to meet his eyes and couldn't. Lowering them, she mumbled. "Okay. I'm a stupid cunt and a cheeky dumb bitch and I accept your offer. I'll... show them to you."

"Say you're a worthless slut or you can get out of my office right now."

Slut. A person who engaged in casual sex with partners.

She could accept being called a cunt and a bitch, because those had no inherent sexual connotations. She could accept having the blonde hair and even getting a boob job, because she knew who she still was on the inside. Her appearance had no bearing on her manner, her deeply-held beliefs.

But calling herself a slut out loud would be admitting that she had sex, that she liked sex, that she wanted sex as often as was humanly possible. And she wasn't so sure anymore what was true and what was not. She did have sex. She liked sex, when it was done right. But did she crave it? Did she get horny over the slightest thing and need satisfaction?

Charlotte thought of touching herself in the shower, and using a dildo on herself, and getting turned on when Mamba forced her to degrade herself.

And she thought back to the occasion that had started all of this, watching Katerina react to the vibrator buried in her pussy. Charlotte's own pussy had twinged, and she thought it was a sympathetic pain. But it could have been arousal.

Did she wish she'd been the one to have that vibrator shaking her to an orgasm?

She didn't know anymore. She couldn't separate out what was the truth and what was a lie. Mamba was changing her, just like he changed all the girls that he eventually hired to work in his businesses.

Tears sprang into her eyes. "I'm a worthless slut," she sobbed.

"Show me your tits."

Lips trembling, Charlotte grabbed her shirt and hiked it up. She pulled it up to her shoulders, pulling one arm out in the process. Her panties were out on display and so was her bra, simple and white with cups that hid her from sight. Her breasts hadn't gone down in size even while she lost weight, so they looked especially full and round. How could they not be good enough for him?

Her hand shook. Charlotte grabbed one of the cups and yanked it up, letting her breast pop out.

Mamba hissed between his teeth. He lifted his phone. "The other one, Charlotte."

She whimpered and sniffled and lifted the other side of her bra, letting her breasts hang free. She felt their weight pressing on her, no longer supported and kept in place by her bra.

Mamba's thumb worked over his phone screen. Charlotte heard each click as he took pictures, the fake sound of a camera shutter snapping. The humiliation went on and on. She thought she might still be standing there in front of him when the world came to an end.

And then it was over. Mamba put his phone down on his desk. "Good cunt. Now get out."

Charlotte yanked at her dress, pulling it down. Her bra and dress tangled up together and she struggled with it for several long seconds before managing to get herself covered again.

"Get out," Mamba repeated, his voice going ragged. He grabbed the girl under his desk and brought her back to his cock, holding her head down on him. The girl writhed against him, sucking and sucking, greedy and eager.

"How will I... The... surgeon?"

"I'll get it set up, free of cost to you. He'll call you with the date and time. You will send proof afterwards. You know the drill."

Of course Mamba has all my information, so it won't be a problem for him to tell the surgeon everything.

Mamba stopped paying attention to her, then. She may as well have ceased to exist. He leaned back in his chair, and held the girl's head, her silver-blonde hair spilling through his fingers. He pumped his hips, thrusting his huge cock into her mouth, and she rode him and fucked him with her mouth.

Charlotte didn't want to witness it.

She turned and fled the office. Just as she reached the door and threw it open, Mamba sucked his breath in sharply and then groaned out.

He's cumming.

Slapping sounds, like something was being banged on the desk. Maybe the girl, as Mamba bucked in ecstasy beneath her. It sounded so wild, so animalistic. Charlotte's pussy gave a sudden throb in response. A thought flew through her mind, forbidden and unbidden.

What would it be like, to have sex like that?

She fled, trying to outrun her own treachery.

Chapter Thirteen

Titty troubles

CHARLOTTE ANSWERED HER PHONE every single time it rang over the next several days, even when she didn't recognize the number. Especially when she didn't recognize the number, since she knew the surgeon friend of Mamba's would be calling her to tell her when her appointment was. It wasn't until then that she realized how many times she was called by spammers and telemarketers, and haters. How those haters acquired her phone number, she would never know, but they had. Either way, she knew that when she answered the phone and the caller was already speaking, raging at her, it was someone come to express their sheer displeasure over her very existence; she ended those calls as soon as they started, beyond the point of defending herself in the eyes of the public.

She couldn't defend herself when she wasn't even quite sure what her real purpose was anymore.

She dreaded every single phone call, tensing whenever her phone screen lit up. No matter what the reason, whether it was her phone telling her she had a low battery, or needed to update, or had a call, she tensed up so hard her muscles began to ache from the constant strain.

It was getting to the point where she didn't know how much more she was going to be able to take. A person had limits. Regular people like her did, at least. This whole thing with Mamba kept pushing her and pushing her and she was already far beyond what she thought she could withstand. She had long since been broken and now, well, now she simply waited to be tossed in the trash once Mamba realized he no longer had a use for her.

She sat in her office chair, gazing blankly at her laptop. It had died while she was working away, searching for options on how to make money, and she couldn't find the energy to get up and fetch the plug from where it lay, coiled, black and snakelike, along the wall. She had been trying to set up a false identity for herself, a pseudonym of sorts she could use to get jobs. Unfortunately, her research had shown her she still needed to prove her actual identity and no one would accept her. It was just as well that she didn't plug the computer in and get it working again, since her latest attempt to recover was looking bleak.

Out of the corner of her eye, Charlotte saw her phone light up. She flinched and braced herself, breath lodging in her throat. A jingling tune, ironically cheerful, accompanied the device's vibration. She could tell from where she sat that the number calling her had no name attached to it, meaning it could have been anyone.

A disgruntled former fan, or a recorded voice attempting to finagle her social security number from her.

Charlotte reached for her phone, her fingers shaking just as much as it was. She picked it up and slid her thumb over the screen to answer the call, an automatic action that didn't at all reflect how tightly her anxieties had wound her, how fast her heart beat.

"Hello?" She sounded normal, without a tremor in her voice, though by that point the shaking extended to the rest of her body.

"Hello, this is Anita at the office of Dr. Richard Johnson. Am I speaking to Charlotte Aria?"

Her heart leaped up into her throat. "Yes," she squeaked.

Maybe, just maybe, her change in tone would reach the woman on the other end of the phone. Maybe Anita would sense something was wrong and reach out to her, become her one and only supporter. She might have connections to other, more powerful people, and could start a chain reaction that eventually led to vindication.

All Anita said was, "Great. I'm just calling to remind you of your appointment on Saturday."

Saturday. Too soon. Much too soon.

"What time?" Charlotte croaked.

Please, hear my voice. Please listen to me, Anita. Something is very wrong and I need someone to help me. Anyone. Get me out of this.

Her desperate fantasy of being rescued by some sort of modern white knight would go unfulfilled. Anita sounded almost bored when she spoke again, a woman reciting a list she had been made to memorize. "Your appointment is at noon. Please show up an hour early to have plenty of time to fill out the forms. Please do not eat for twelve hours before the surgery, though make sure to stay hydrated. That's about it."

Charlotte licked her lips. "Where is the clinic?"

That seemed to throw Anita for a loop, pulling her out of her script. "You'll be having your surgery at the Memorial Hospital."

A hospital, where dozens of people would see her. She had been hoping to have this done at a plastic surgery clinic, as strange as that sounded when put in context with the rest of her hopes. Fewer people would be at a specialized clinic. But a general hospital? She would draw so much attention. The thought of starting another frenzy like the one at the job fair terrified her and filled her with shame.

Her heavy breathing echoed into the phone.

Anita hung up, perhaps eager to get out of the conversation after its weird turn. Charlotte set her phone down and put her head in her hands. She had become quite a bit more imaginative in the several months since she lost the trial to Mamba and could picture easily how things would proceed from here. Blissfully unaware of Charlotte's identity, Anita would look into her as a curiosity project, goaded on by wondering what sort of woman scheduled a breast augmentation surgery without knowing where she would be having it done. Anita would be then dropped into the rabbit hole of hate and loathing Charlotte had unwittingly dug for herself.

Charlotte's only consolation, and it was a pitiful one indeed, was that Anita worked at the clinic and would not be at the hospital to see her.

Charlotte pulled out of her daydreaming and shook her head at herself. The reality was so much worse than anything she could conjure up. She was nothing. A no one. Whether Anita learned who she was or not didn't matter. Charlotte was nothing, had nothing.

She got into her car at 9:30 on Saturday, stomach empty, mouth dry despite the copious amount of water she had been drinking to have something to occupy her fiddling hands. She arrived at the hospital at 9:50 and parked in the outpatient lot, in the farthest spot back she could find. Climbing out of the car with her purse, she strolled off through the parking lot, toward the pristine and imposing castle that was the hospital, trying to make the journey last as long as possible.

The sound of a car door shutting, almost right in her ear, brought her flinching around. A woman with natural golden blonde hair looked over her shoulder at her, hands still on the handle of the liftgate on the back of her van. She grimaced. "Sorry. I didn't see you."

"It's okay," Charlotte started to say.

A much older woman, idling nearby in a wheelchair, zipped up with a few strokes of her wheel, running right up on Charlotte's little toe. "Don't talk to her, Susan!" the old woman croaked. She raised her gnarled hand and pointed a branchlike and knobby finger into Charlotte's face. "She's the little prude who thinks she's too good to suck cock!"

Charlotte turned and walked away, incapable of comprehending what had happened. Never in her life would she have imagined hearing those words coming from the mouth of an elderly, supposedly respectable woman.

Inside the hospital wasn't any better. People turned to stare at her as she passed and normal conversations ended with an abruptness, replaced by whispers that simply had to be about her, having no other explanation. Charlotte ducked her head to hide behind her long, pale hair and walked faster, though she had up until then been trying to make the moments last.

Only when she was striding through the halls, purposeless, did she realize that she didn't actually know where she was supposed to go. Stopping, she looked around, and saw the sign for an information desk.

No. I don't want to have to talk to someone. Not like this.

She told herself to use her brain. Where would a woman go to have a surgery like this? Not cardiology. Not radiology.

She looked around a bit more and found a directory not far from the information desk sign. Scanning through the list, she came across Cosmetic Surgery. That had to be it.

Charlotte took a peek at the map and then worked her way from where she was to the cosmetology department, on the second floor. She walked inside the room and went up to the desk.

A very large and very black woman peered at her over her glasses. "Sign in, please."

Charlotte reached for the pen on the window ledge.

The large woman laughed. "Just kidding, honey. Do you see anyone else in here?"

"No," Charlotte replied, after a cursory glance around. She had been so intent on not being noticed that she'd ignored her surroundings and hadn't noticed she'd wandered into a completely empty waiting room.

"You're Charlotte, right?"

"Yes."

"Take these forms and go fill them out for me. After that, we'll be able to get you on your way!"

Charlotte grabbed the clipboard handed to her through the window and carried it over to a seat as far away from the foreboding door to the back as was possible. That was where the bad things would happen.

The papers on the clipboard, at first, were similar to the ones she had filled out at doctor's offices before. Her name, address, social security number, and birth date were all required in a few places. It got worse after that. She had to list any diseases and disabilities in her immediate family, and any diseases she herself might have, or conditions that might complicate the surgery. Looking at those blank spaces, available for her to fill in with a variety of ailments, reminded her just how real this was.

It wasn't a nightmare.

She was actually going to have to do this.

There wasn't much for her to do in that section.

The next one required her to write down the names and numbers of some emergency contacts. Perhaps knowing she would have none, Mamba had gone ahead and had someone add him as a contact.

One more page and it was a final release form, stating she gave approval for the surgery and accepted all the potential risks and ramifications.

As if she had anything left to lose.

Charlotte signed.

Upon receipt of the clipboard, a slender nurse appeared and guided Charlotte to a private room with a bed and a curtained bathroom area. Under her instruction, Charlotte stripped and secured her clothes in a bag for later, and then got dressed in one of those skimpy hospital gowns that left the back open. She could feel the cold air on her ass, sliding between her legs.

Practically naked, she was led to a small room that might have been comfortable if not for the examination equipment lining the oaken countertops, spilling suggestively out from behind the cupboard doors.

"Take a seat on the chair," the nurse told her. "Dr. Richard will be here soon to see you."

Charlotte nodded.

She waited until she was alone to sit and then plopped down on the chair. It reminded her of a dentist's chair, yet plusher and with a headrest that felt much more like a pillow than it probably should have. She closed her tired eyes and knitted her fingers together over her stomach. Then, slid her hands a little lower, as if trying to hide her genitals. She had always been a bit self-conscious about the shape of her pussy because her labia was longer than what she considered to be normal, and sitting naked in a hospital made her very aware of her private parts. Her bare, naked ass was right on the cushy chair, after all.

The door opened. She almost jumped out of her skin from the shock of it. A very tall and handsome man strode in, a huge bulge in his tight white pants leading the way. Charlotte almost fainted at the sight of his package. She had never seen such a massive cock before. It absolutely had to be massive from the way it thrust forward at the crotch of his pants, so heavy he had to wear a belt to keep its weight from pushing them down over time.

The man walked right over to Charlotte, putting his bulge almost in her face. He extended his smooth hand to her. "Charlotte. I'm Dr. Johnson. You can just call me Dick."

A more apt nickname had never existed.

Charlotte took his hand, blinking hard. She had to assume his huge "Johnson" was the result of plastic surgery or some sort of enhancement. Dr. Richard Johnson was clearly into what he had on offer, with a pristine straight nose and a sculpted chin and cheekbones that were utterly, and literally, unreal. With the way he styled his hair, he resembled a porn version of Ken from Barbie.

"Let's see what we're working with here," Dr. Johnson said. He took hold of Charlotte's gown and pulled it forward and down. Her breasts popped out, jiggling from the force of the movement.

Charlotte stared down at herself in abject horror. She felt like a woman in a movie, but also as if she was watching the film of herself. She could both feel and see herself feel in what must have been a sort of out-of-body experience.

Dr. Johnson reached for her breasts and fondled them, squeezing them in his warm hands. He ran his fingers all over her, rasping them over her sensitive nipples. He pulled a deep and squeezing sort of massage that ended up with her areolas pinched between all of his fingers.

Tears sparked in Charlotte's eyes. She bit her lip, struggling to restrain them.

"These are some nice tits you've got, Charlotte," Dr. Johnson purred to her. "But they could be so much nicer. And that's why you're here. That's why Mamba sent you to me."

She couldn't help it. She sniffled.

Dr. Johnson leaned over her, his cock bulge pushing on her. He whispered into her ear, "No one will ever believe you about anything. I can do whatever I want to you."

She sobbed.

Dr. Johnson leaned back and resumed feeling her breasts all over. His voice returned to neutral. "Luckily, you came to me. You know you need the best and I got it for you. When I'm through with you, you'll have the most amazing pair of titties in the whole city."

"Thank you, Sir," she whimpered.

He laughed aloud and got up from his chair. "I like that. Mamba's been doing some good work with you. Well, let's get this show on the road."

Almost as if arriving on cue, a nurse opened the door, showing a flash of Charlotte's breasts to the several people outside the room. The nurse pulled a piece of equipment after her, severely delaying shutting the door. Charlotte's cheeks burned and she lowered her head in shame.

The nurse set up her machine while Dr. Johnson fiddled around with Charlotte's breasts, making an occasional contemplative sound. She could tell from how hard he dug his fingers into her that it was all for show, that he didn't need to be doing this.

She didn't need to be doing this.

She could go. No one was stopping her.

Charlotte opened her mouth to protest, to call a halt to this whole thing.

The nurse straightened up with a syringe in her hand. "We're ready, Doctor."

Dr. Johnson let Charlotte's breasts drop from his hands. They bounced around freely from the drop, pulling at her. "Okay. Charlotte, this injection is just a general anesthetic. That means it's going to put you to sleep. Don't worry. When you wake up, you're going to be beautiful."

I already am beautiful, she wanted to cry.

The nurse slid the needle into her vein in one practiced motion and depressed the syringe plunger. A strange tingling burn surged through Charlotte and then she fell sideways, into unrelenting darkness so deep and empty it was euphoric.

For a time, she thought of nothing, did nothing. She didn't exist, in an even more thorough way than Mamba had caused.

She blinked and stared at a ceiling overhead long before she became aware of waking up. A strange pain, an aching heaviness, gripped her chest region. Charlotte lifted her arm and saw some sort of drip attached to her, another needle in her vein, right next to the bruises left by the first. She lowered her arm, a sluggish and dreamlike movement. Tilting her head, she looked down and saw the way the blanket covering her body rose up in hills over her breasts, much larger and rounder than what she was used to, than what she knew her body to look like.

She started shaking.

Charlotte took hold of the blanket and lifted it up. Her breasts were there, exactly where they should be, exactly like what they should look like. Smooth skin, pink nipples. However, they were twice the size they should have been.

No.

Charlotte reached and grabbed the drip needle and tore it from her wrist. Blood beaded up. She ignored it and sat up with a huge effort, dragging herself to the edge of the bed. Standing, the world tilted around her before returning to a somewhat normal orientation. She staggered to the wall of the room she was in and followed it around until she came to a curtained area, another bathroom. A mirror re-flected her bed, the dangling needle hanging from a bag of anonymous fluid.

Charlotte reached out and fumbled, flipping the light switch.

Now she could see herself, just a snatch of her face in the corner. She shuffled over to get a better look and saw a woman that she didn't recognize, a buxom blonde with big–huge–perfect tits and a head of tousled, flowing blonde hair.

The woman in the mirror was a purely sexual creature, the dream girl who appeared in every man's sleeping fantasies.

Charlotte ran her hands down over her body and the minx in the mirror mimicked her, trailing her fingers sensually from her enormous breasts to her flat stomach and full hips. A tingle formed deep in her sex and she gasped, shaking. The quiver hurt her, her augmented breasts throbbing. She pressed her hands to them, shocked out of the hypnotic trance that had come over her. She had, for a second there, fallen into the delusion Mamba wanted her to believe.

"No!" she cried out.

The door to her room burst open and a nurse barged in, her face etched with a deep grimace. She noticed Charlotte and ran up behind her. Charlotte watched in the mirror as the nurse came up to her and grabbed her, holding her around the shoulders.

"What are you doing out of bed?" the nurse scolded. "And you ripped out your drip!"

"What happened to me?" Charlotte whispered.

The nurse tugged on her and turned her around, guiding her back to the bed. "Nothing happened," the nurse soothed, misunderstanding. "We noticed you were a little dehydrated, so we gave you a saline drip. Everything's okay. Your surgery went fine. You'll be able to go home soon, but you need to rest so you don't hurt yourself."

What she had allowed to be done to herself hurt her more than enough.

Chapter Fourteen

Flappy flaps

CHARLOTTE STOOD IN FRONT of the big mirror in her bathroom, holding her breasts in her hands. She lifted them up, moved them around, searching for a sign of the surgery. At last, she spotted two small cuts, closed up with tiny stitches, in the fold of skin where her breasts connected to her chest. They were hardly noticeable, though she'd gone through the surgery only three hours ago.

Dr. Richard was very good at what he did.

Her breasts were tender and moving too quickly made her wince. She couldn't help poking and prodding a bit though, trying to feel the silicone implants underneath the natural form. She couldn't.

Looking at herself, she couldn't see any sign that her hair had once been anything but blonde.

Who she was and who Mamba wanted her to be were melding into one.

She closed her eyes and put her hand to her face.

A few days later, she received the usual notification in the mail, stating that her payment had been waived. She was freed, released for another month, which meant it was time for her to begin her frantic search for some form of monetary gain. Charlotte went and sat down in her office and pulled up a listing of jobs throughout the entire state. She couldn't legally leave the state until she paid off her debt, unless she went through Mamba and he gave her approval through the court system, but that didn't prevent her from heading out within its boundaries to chase a job.

The words marched around in front of her, a meaningless trail of ants.

Charlotte leaned back in her chair, her huge new breasts shifting up higher on her chest, aching.

Suddenly, she knew she couldn't kid herself anymore.

She had gone back and forth all these months between accepting her fate and scheming to get out of her predicament. It was time to stop playing games. She had to grow up and admit she would never get out of this. She would never be rescued or find a way to rescue herself. She was stuck in this, unrecognizable from when she began, and there wasn't a single thing she could do about it.

Looking as she did, no one would hire her even if she wasn't public enemy number one. She looked like a whore, a bimbo, a slacker. She looked like she hadn't a single brain cell in her head and couldn't type properly or speak clearly or even make coffee without fucking up.

She looked like a brain-dead sex-machine.

The only way for her to make money would be through selling herself, and she refused.

She refused to show herself to the world.

For the next month, she simply didn't leave her apartment. Everything she needed, she bought online and had shipped to her. Even food. She retrieved her packages in the dead of night when she had no chance of being spotted. Living as she did in a less desirable area now, sometimes her packages were stolen. Money lost, wasted.

She didn't have it in her to care anymore.

She made her usual return to Mamba's office. He sat behind his desk, waiting for her with a sharp grin uncoiled on his lips.

Charlotte lowered her head, knowing that he saw her as an extension of the pornographic images on his walls. She was useless, an object, pointless and purposeless without him.

She... needed him.

"Good morning, sir," Charlotte said quietly. She clasped her hands together. "I'm back again. I can't pay you this month. I'm... a stupid cunt."

The words stung far less when they came from her own mouth without him having forced them. They almost tasted like freedom, like choice.

Mamba grinned wider and leaned forward over his desk. "Stupid cunts don't wear clothes. Show me what I paid for."

A flush of humiliation brought color to her cheeks. She didn't resist, though. She'd gone beyond that.

"Stupid cunts don't wear clothes," she agreed.

First to go was her oversized jacket, bought cheap online, which she had been using to hide her big tits. Next to go was her shirt and bra, leaving her breasts out on display.

Mamba let out a deep purring sound. "Amazing. Dr. Dick has done a fantastic job on you, as always. Lift up your tits. Let me see."

Charlotte held her heavy breasts in her hands and lifted them.

Mamba tilted his head and nodded to himself. "No scar. Fantastic. You are a perfect woman now, in appearance."

She forced herself not to say anything in response. She used to tell her young audience to love themselves despite any flaws they might have, or believe they had. Mamba suggesting a scar would have made her imperfect was just another strike against what she believed in. She was getting used to that by now.

"Keep going, stupid cunt."

Charlotte looked at him for mercy, found none. She peeled off her skirt and panties, letting them puddle on the ground around her heels. She kicked the clothes aside and stood there, nude, exposed.

Other than Dr. Richard Johnson–Dr. Dick, as Mamba called him, very aptly–no one had seen her naked in a long time. Charlotte flexed her fingers, struggling against the urge to cover her pussy with her hands. She was hairless down there, not for any sexual reason but because she liked the smooth feeling. She'd gone through laser hair removal years ago.

It wasn't the nakedness of her pussy that made her flush and turn pink, however. It was her large labia. What would he think of her huge pussy lips, laying so long and moist against her inner thighs?

Mamba looked her over with painful intensity, his eyes raking over her body. She stood there and took it as he fucked her with his eyes, ogling her huge tits and her big pussy lips. He clearly liked what he saw, what she had become. Except, as time dragged on, as she waited, naked before him, he focused more and more of his attention on her pussy than on the rest of her. His stare wasn't his typical glower, his glare of disapproval and judgment; rather, he seemed to approve. Relief pulsed through her, followed by a hotter spasm of what could only be called arousal. Finally, there was some part of her that he liked, that he wouldn't change, a part of her that was hers and absolutely natural, even if she was ashamed of it.

Her nipples stiffened, protruding from her round breasts. A slight warmth throbbed in her pussy, making her inner muscles clench. She felt herself getting a little wet and struggled to get her mind onto other subjects, knowing her flappy pussy lips would clearly show to Mamba the effect he was having upon her. Yet, in the back of her mind, a traitorous little voice whispered that, as she no longer had any reason to resist, it would be easier to give in. The little voice whispered that he was fucking her with his eyes, and that now she was his perfect woman, he might want to fuck her for real.

Charlotte's breath caught in her throat.

Her pussy got wetter, trickles of her aroused juices leaking from her, working their way down the inside of her lips.

She wondered what it would feel like to be fucked by him. She had seen a glimpse of his cock and it was huge, though not a false monster like what Dr. Dick harbored in his pants. He was a natural man, and he probably had a lot of skill, given his line of work.

Her eyes half-shut as she pictured his thick cock pushed into her pussy, her big lips dragging along his length as he plunged in and out of her.

"You have the biggest cuntflaps I have ever seen."

Charlotte jerked out of her fantasy and flushed scarlet. Far from sounding smitten with her, Mamba spoke in his usual neutral hiss.

"Damn, I've seen a lot in my day. But I haven't seen everything."

Charlotte ducked her head, biting her lip. *Stupid, stupid. How could you ever think he would approve of you?*

"Does that embarrass you? You don't like your flappy cuntflaps?"

"Please," she whispered. "Sir. I'm a stupid dumb cunt with cuntflaps and I need your help. I need you to give me another month."

Mamba sat back in his chair and folded his hands together over his firm stomach. "What a stupid cunt. You've had every chance and still you haven't made anything of yourself. Look at you. What a waste. You aren't even trying."

She had been trying so hard, but she didn't dare argue with him.

"You're pathetic." He looked at her coolly, like she was nothing more than a mouse before his might. "I can see I still have much work to do on you before you finally understand."

"I'll do anything, sir. I swear I will."

A thin smile played on his lips. "You swear it. By what? What do you have to swear on? You have nothing."

"My body."

"Your body isn't yours any longer. Your body belongs to me." Mamba flashed a darker grin than before. "But you know that. I can see it in your eyes. I think you might be ready."

"Are you going to... have sex with me?"

"You don't feel like you've been fucked over enough already?" Mamba burst out laughing at her.

Charlotte put her hands to her face, hiding behind them.

"I have an offer to make you. I will get rid of the rest of your debt, free you from having to pay me money if you do one thing for me."

Charlotte's heart jumped with her relief. One more thing. One more humiliating task, that was all she had to get through and then she would be freed.

"I want you to work for me, Charlotte."

She didn't understand at first. "What?"

"Work for me, stupid dumb bitch. Is that so hard to understand?" Mamba's nostrils flared, his dark eyes blazing. "I will give you your old job back under the condition that you make videos only about the subjects I want you to cover. I will reinstate all your social media and give you your life back in exchange for your work." He grinned. "As long as you work for me, I will let you do whatever else you want with your life. But the moment you dare even think of betraying me, you will regret it. You will find yourself in a situation even worse than this one right now."

"You... my job?" Her mind raced. Her legs trembled, making her feel as if she might collapse to the ground. "My old job? You'll... I will get paid?"

"Yes, bitch." Mamba smirked. "Everything will go back to normal for you. It will almost seem as if you have traveled back in time to the point right before you decided to challenge me. Hopefully, you will have learned from your mistakes and will do what you know is best. That is, if you accept my offer."

"If I don't?" she dared to ask.

"This is the final time I want to see you here in my office. I'm getting tired of this arrangement. Either you agree and take your old job back, or you will go to prison for not paying me."

She knew that she had no choice. While it would be absolutely awful to work with him and make the terrible sorts of videos he wanted, she couldn't help but feel that it would be worth it just to get her life back. Part of being an adult and a successful businessperson was doing things that had to be done, whether they were desirable or not.

"I accept," she said.

"You accept what?"

Charlotte gave herself a mental slap and steadied herself. "I would love to have my job back, sir, if you will give it to me."

"Good cunt. You can have your job. I'll send you the details soon. Now
get out of my office."

"Thank you," Charlotte whispered. She bent and snatched up her
clothes, forgetting herself in her relief. Her breasts bounced, her
swollen and wet labia jiggling.

Mamba laughed aloud with delight and clapped his hands, a slow and
mocking clap that followed her even as she fled, half-dressed, from his
office.

Chapter Fifteen

How low can you go?

MAMBA EMAILED HER EARLY the next morning, somehow having gotten access to the new address she'd been forced to set up after he took the old one down. The email was short, brief, and to the point. To be briefed on the requirements of her job, she was to drive to him at his mansion on the outskirts of the city. And because this was Mamba, he couldn't make it easy on her. He included the stipend that, to be accepted for her job, she had to be dressed properly. That was, not dressed at all.

Charlotte reread the last couple of sentences, her lips moving, struggling to make sense of them. "When you are five miles from my home, you stop and get out of your vehicle and strip down to nothing. When you show up at my front door, you must be wet. I will know if you do not follow these instructions exactly."

In order to be wet, she would have to masturbate. Masturbating while driving sounded extremely dangerous. She bit her lip, debating on arguing the point with him. She'd masturbate in front of him if he wanted, but to risk her life fucking herself while in a speeding vehicle?

Then again, she wasn't kidding anyone. She'd had her head doused in bleach and went under the scalpel at his bequest. She had been risking her health for him this whole time in order to meet his ridiculous demands. This was no different. If she got in a wreck, then she would no longer have to worry about pleasing him, and he wouldn't have to pay her for a job she would most likely suck at. She almost wondered if he intended for her to get in an accident and perish, if that was his true plan. A man like him could have someone killed rather easily, but he was more subtle than that. He wanted her to be ashamed even when she died, pulled naked and with her fingers still in her pussy from the wreckage.

She didn't get in a wreck but she was ashamed regardless of what she was doing when, on the way to his home, she reached the point where she would need to pleasure herself if she wanted to be wet for him by the time she arrived.

Charlotte removed one hand from her steering wheel and right away found her car canting to the left, her grip unbalanced. She quickly fixed herself, getting all four tires back within the lines, her heart pounding hard in her chest, beating on her rib cage. She never even ate while driving, or drank, and hardly ever fiddled with the radio, preferring to listen to a series of endless blue jazz CDs. This was the first time she would be intentionally distracting herself.

Charlotte dropped her speed by five miles and put on cruise control, hedging her bets. She put her hand on her crotch and rubbed herself through the material of her pants. Her full lips filled out the material, stretching it. By running her fingers over the thin denim, she could feel the shape of herself.

She was dry as a bone, her pussy as still as a rock carving.

Using her one hand, she undid the button on her jeans and pulled the zipper down. She pushed her hand inside her panties and slid her fingers through her warm, dry slit. Not so much as a tingle occurred.

"Come on," she growled, pushing her fingers against her pussy, rubbing vigorously up and down, still to no result. She was getting nearer to Mamba's road, the side street that led away from the highway. The street was little more than five miles long, which meant she needed to also get naked soon. Time was running out for her.

Charlotte tried to think of the times when she had been horny recently and what had gotten it started. Running through the options, she found herself fixating on that first moment, when she watched Katrina writhing around on the couch, at the mercy of the vibrator inside her.

Maybe she should have brought along a sex toy, but the only one she had was a dildo and she would really wreck the car if she had to thrust a dildo inside herself. A vibrator would have been better. Too bad that the only thing vibrating right now was her car.

My car.

An idea came to her, so devilish and naughty that she knew it would work.

Mamba's road was ahead, in the distance, meandering away from the highway and past scrubby meadows to a wooded area.

Charlotte flipped on her emergency flashers and pulled off onto the side of the road. Cars blasted by her in both directions. One coming her way honked at her, while another seemed on the verge of slowing down to assist her before speeding off again.

Her stomach was in knots as she climbed out of her car, standing on the grassy shoulder of the road. She couldn't see cars for quite a ways in either direction.

Now was her chance.

Charlotte stripped off her clothes faster than she ever had before, until she stood naked on the roadside, bared to the elements. The wind caressed her thighs, and the sun shone on her big breasts, turning her smooth skin golden.

A car appeared, approaching rapidly.

Charlotte threw herself back into the driver's seat, her heart beating rapidly. She started driving again, picking up speed. Turning off the highway, the road type changed, going from a paved and maintained speedway to a bumpy mess. The vibration in her car ramped up as the wheels bounced, jostled all over.

Excited now, her plan in execution, Charlotte leaned forward so that her pussy rested firmly on the seat. Vibrations pulsed from her car and straight to her pussy, jiggling her labia and reaching straight to her core. A moan rolled from her throat, it felt so good. She couldn't believe she had never done anything like this before. Breathless, she pushed her fingers back to her pussy and rubbed her outer lips. Little jolts of static rocked through her. Her hips bucked in spasm.

Charlotte moved her hand further down and ground her clit. Her juices ran, gathering hot in the palm of her hand. She arched her back, thrusting out her breasts, rubbing on herself.

The roar of another engine approaching barely reached her. Charlotte forced herself to focus on the road, though she could no longer gather the strength to remove her hand from her crotch. She drove on, rubbing her pussy, while a truck trundled on toward her.

Silently, she begged the driver not to pay attention to her.

As she should have learned by then, begging did nothing. The truck driver slowed down upon approaching her. A man in a cowboy hat leaned his head out the window and stared at her as they passed, ogling the naked, big-breasted, blonde-haired slut who was so horny she had to fuck herself while she drove. That, at least, was all he would see, all he would understand.

Charlotte pushed the encounter from her mind and focused on the task at hand, letting the car's vibrations carry her deeper and deeper into sexual degradation.

Mamba's home appeared from out of the woodland, a behemoth perversion of Victorian architecture with off-white with blue-black roofing, edged with spikes and pillars and spirals. It was an imposing den perfectly suited to a snake-like Mamba.

Charlotte parked out in front of his grotesque house. At least there were no other houses around, no neighbors who could gawk at her without her knowing. Holding her keys in her hand, since she had no pockets now in which to put them, she walked up to his front door and rang the bell.

The door opened in an instant, as if he had been standing on the other side awaiting her. She had never been so close to him before and was taken aback all over again about how imposing he was. She'd gotten so used to him sitting behind that desk, but now he was standing over her, looking at her with contempt down the bridge of his nose. He wore a shimmering black blazer over a thin white shirt that showed off his muscular body, and a belt studded with what could only be real emeralds.

Mamba moved, so swiftly she didn't know what was happening until it was too late. He took her keys from her and put them in his pocket.

"Who are you?"

"Charlotte, sir." This game she knew by now.

Mamba shook his head. "You're mistaken. Charlotte is a pathetic bitch. Your name is Cuntflaps."

She gasped and took a step back, feeling like he had slapped her. She twisted away from him, and then turned back, knowing she couldn't leave. Her car was locked, and he had the key. She couldn't even get her clothes back, much less drive away.

She turned back to face him, her head so low her chin almost touched her breasts. The initial shock of being called Cuntflaps faded, leaving her with a bit of clarity. "Charlotte is a pathetic bitch." Not, "You're a pathetic bitch."

By calling her that name, was he telling her he approved of her more in her current state? If she went by Cuntflaps, would she be accepting his approval?

She had to try, no matter how terrible it felt.

"You're right, sir. I'm sorry, sir. My name is Cuntflaps. I'm naked and wet, just like you asked. I hope... you like it."

"Spread," he instructed.

Charlotte spread her legs. Her juices, freed, ran down her inner thighs and almost all the way to her ankles. The warm wetness felt so good, pouring through her pussy like that, trickling over her, well, her cuntflaps.

Mamba reached to her and pushed two of his fingers into her slit. He brought them back out and smeared her own juices on her cheek. The musky scent of her own lust caught in her nostrils. "Good cunt. Come in."

Charlotte followed him inside, leaving her pussy juices to dry on her cheek.

Inside, the house proved to be no less intimidating than the outside. Mamba led her through a vast and cavernous foyer to a massive living room almost the size of his executive office. Bronze pillars sprouted like trees from the floor, bursting up to connect with the ceiling. Huge plush couches sat on the real wooden flooring, around a black glass coffee table. Lights rimmed a recessed ceiling. At one end was a fireplace, casting an eerie play of light and shadow across half the room. The hairs on the back of Charlotte's neck stood up. She felt, quite sharply, deeply, that this wasn't a place where she belonged. There was a masculinity to the place, a lack of decorations that went beyond simply spartan. The absence was... threatening.

Nowhere to hide.

"Sit," Mamba said, pointing at one of his massive couches. Other than the cushions that belonged there, the couch in question, and the others lacked comfort. Not a single throw pillow or quilt was in sight.

Charlotte sat.

Mamba took up a seat on the other couch opposite her, far across the coffee table. "For your videos, you will be following an exact script from now on. I know that, before, you were allowed to research your own subjects. That didn't work out well. From now on, you will be given a script, and you are to do exactly what is written on it. You will wear what you are told to wear and say exactly what you are told to say. I will not be so lenient with you as Damien was. Everything you do will be overseen by me. If it isn't right, you will do it again, over and over until you meet my standards. Are we clear on that?"

"Yes, sir," she said. If that was the worst of it, then so be it. She could follow directions. It was better to be humiliated than go to jail.

"You will be filming your first video today, in my home studio." His eyes flashed. "How well your video performs is up to you. If you want to make any money, you had best give it your all."

A question crawled up the back of her throat, but she swallowed it down.

Mamba must have seen the look on her face, though. "Yes, you will get paid. You are getting your job back exactly as you left it. The arrangement is as it stands. Following the publication of your first video, the one you will film today, I will then erase your debt. Here is the script."

He picked up a piece of paper that had been laying on the couch and pushed it over in her direction, across the smooth coffee table.

Charlotte picked it up, though didn't yet look at it. Mamba wasn't done speaking.

"You will film one video per day, every day. Later on, Cuntflaps, if you're good, I might allow you to have a day off."

"Thank you, sir."

"Through all of this, you will be expected to keep up your appearance. If I spot one brown root on your head, you will go to a hair salon immediately and return afterward to film the video. I don't care how long it takes. Do you understand?"

"Yes, sir."

"Good cunt. Now, take a look at your script."

Charlotte flipped the paper over. The title at the very top read "How to Enjoy Degrading Sex."

The urge to roll her eyes was so real. She closed her eyes and waited until she had herself under control.

He wanted her to go back on everything she had said, no doubt. This was only the beginning. He would want her to promote the slut lifestyle and vouch for his clubs, his programs, his betrayals to womanhood.

She had no choice.

Mamba slapped his hand down on the coffee table, making her jump. "You can't read with your fucking eyes closed."

"I'm sorry," she whispered, and lowered her eyes to the script.

"You had best start taking this seriously, Cuntflaps. There's no more chances after this."

Frightened, she got to reading.

Chapter Sixteen

Try harder

CHARLOTTE FINISHED READING THROUGH what Mamba wanted her to say in his video. She had been so certain she couldn't get any lower, but, as it turned out, she was wrong.

She set the script aside and leaned back on the couch, not caring for once that this position made her fake breasts push forward and really stand out.

"What do you think, Cuntflaps?"

What do I think?

She was dizzy, sickened by the reality of what she was going to be doing. Doing things privately for Mamba was one thing. Humiliating, degrading, but she had managed it. Making this video would be using her fame to broadcast horrible, humiliating things to her young and impressionable audience.

"Cuntflaps, you had better not be ignoring me." Mamba's voice took on a note of warning.

Sick to her stomach and still dizzy, Charlotte forced herself to sit up. "It's very evocative, sir," she murmured, which was the closest to a compliment she could give.

"It is. I know. I had it written by the very best in the business." He bared his teeth in a smile. "The week after you tried to defy me. It would have been done sooner, but it took time to find the right person."

He had been expecting this all along. For some reason, that didn't shock her. He would have won out against her no matter what.

"But the script is pointless without someone to read it. You must be the evocative one, Cuntflaps. I've seen your older videos. I know there's passion in you somewhere. Let's see if you can put it to good use for once."

"Yes, sir."

Mamba stood, unfolding his muscular body to his great height. "I'll take you to my studio. Come with me."

"Yes, sir," Charlotte intoned, standing up to follow him.

He stood there, glaring at her. "Try again."

She froze, not sure for a moment what he was asking for. She trembled, trying to think of how she could please him.

Mamba's glare went harsh, paralyzing. "What did I just say to you?"

Evocative. Passionate.

Charlotte understood in a snap. She blurted out with much more force, "Yes, sir!"

He laughed and shook his head and she froze again, not sure why he was still disapproving of her. Then, he moved on, leaving her standing there in the middle of his huge living room while he went off. She didn't want to be alone and, even more than that, didn't want to get him mad at her for being slow. She hurried off after him, following him through vast, bare halls in which the only decorations were mirrors hanging on the walls. Charlotte focused on Mamba's back to keep from looking at her naked reflection over and over.

Mamba guided her to a spiraling, glassy staircase and down another set of halls, from which other halls and doors branched off. She was dizzy again, though now from the sheer size of the place. How did he ever know where he was going in here?

Eventually, he brought her to one door out of many and held it open for her. "Step inside."

Charlotte edged into the room and looked around. The recording studio in front of her greatly reminded her of the sets at CM, a real room at one end, studded with cameras and recording software at the other. It looked like a lounge, with a huge red couch and a golden carpet to match with the shimmering red-and-yellow wallpaper.

Charlotte had seen porn only once in her entire life, enough for her to decide she hated it and would never, ever advocate it. Even from that one viewing, she knew that this set-up reminded her of a stage in a porn flick.

"You may be wondering why I have a studio in my own house."

Charlotte nodded in a demure manner. Mamba sounded almost conversational right now.

The wealthy man surveyed his domain with pride, pulling the studio door shut behind him. "I do have some activities outside of the office. Most of them are for my own pleasure, but you will find me on *some* websites online." He paused and tilted his head, rubbing his chin. "Maybe I'll make you watch some of them for research purposes. Now, it's time for you to get dressed in the proper attire so you can shoot your video."

"My clothes are in my car still."

"Dumb bitch," he said, almost fondly. "You aren't going to wear any of that boring crap you fill your closet with. Let me show you my dressing room."

Mamba took her over to a door at the other end of the studio, behind all the camera equipment. He opened the door, revealing what was actually a real dressing room, like the kind famous celebrities and actors got. Massive mirrors hung on the walls, looking over a fantastical quantity of every kind of makeup a woman could imagine. Rack upon rack of clothes framed the back wall, creating yet another maze.

He really likes to confuse and mystify.

She hardly cared. She was so glad she was going to get to wear clothes that she was beside herself.

Mamba crossed the room to one of the clothing racks. Charlotte followed eagerly. The assortment of dresses and gowns gave her so much hope.

"This one will do," Mamba said. He grabbed a very small piece of clothing and thrust it at Charlotte, pushing it into her hands.

Charlotte gaped at the scrap of cloth he'd given her. She held it up in front of her, her hopes sinking again like a punctured balloon. He had handed her a filmy white tube top, barely big enough to cover her breasts and not much else. She stretched the fabric and gasped in horror as she was able to see her hands through the thin mesh of fibers.

"Is... this it?"

"That's it. Put it on and then join me in the studio again. Don't bother playing with any of the makeup. Your face is fine as it is."

She blinked. "Really?"

He grabbed a handful of her blonde hair and swatted at her face with the ends. "Trust me, if it wasn't, I would have had Dr. Dick perform more miracles upon you."

Mamba released her and left the dressing room, left her stunned and a little uncomprehending. Had he complimented her just now, in his own way?

Charlotte held up the tube top and sighed. She pulled it on, struggling to get it over her big breasts. The fabric stretched so tight it turned nearly transparent, showing off a significant amount of detail. The coral pink circlets of her nipples were clearly visible, and that was in addition to the way they jutted out.

There was nothing else for her to do, since her face was "fine as it was." She left the dressing room. Mamba stood behind one of the cameras. His eyes pierced through her as soon as she came into view.

"Sit down on the couch."

Charlotte obeyed. As she walked, she made note of the fact that, though the tightness of the tube top left her so exposed she might as well not have been wearing anything at all, it did keep her breasts nicely contained. They didn't bounce around so much. It was almost a good feeling, a security of sorts that was so difficult to find in her life now.

Because of all the lights shining in her face, she couldn't really see the other half of the room, or Mamba, though her eyes quickly adjusted. The warmth of the stage lights all blasting down upon her was almost comforting in its familiarity, though.

Screw it, she decided. If Mamba wanted a show, she would make sure he got one.

Charlotte spread her legs. Her big pussy lips spread apart, showing off her inner folds. She didn't quite know what to do with her hands and settled for resting them on her thighs.

"You can begin at any time," Mamba told her.

"Don't you want to... check the audio?"

A deathly silence followed her words. She was reminded of a rattlesnake having gone silent, so she couldn't figure out where not to step.

"I'm sorry," she apologized quickly. "I shouldn't question you, sir. I'm a stupid dumb bitch named Cuntflaps. Please forgive me. Please."

A low chuckle met her apology.

Her panic began to fade immediately. Somehow, she was becoming tuned into his shifting moods.

"Whenever you're ready, Cuntflaps."

Charlotte pulled in a deep breath and sat back a little bit, as she used to when making her videos. She put on as good of a smile as she could manage.

"Hi everyone," she said. "And welcome back to Living, Loving, Lifestyling, the most positive and encouraging channel you'll ever come across. I'm your host, Charlotte. Here at Triple L, we're all about making dreams come true."

Her old intro slid so neatly from her lips. She trembled with relief. It felt so damn good to be working, no matter what form it took.

Now, onto the script Mamba had written.

"I'm sorry that I've been gone for so long. I had to take a break for my mental health. When I posted my last video, I wasn't in a very good place and it made me say things that I shouldn't have. I feel so much better now though, and I've had a lot of time to think about what I did." Going off-script, Charlotte added, "It's almost like I'm a whole different person now."

"You might be noticing that I'm in a different place, and that my hair is different, and that I've gotten a boob job. There are so many new and wonderful things that I have to tell you about. Let's start with the obvious. I don't have any pants on. I'm sitting here showing off my pussy to you to let you know I'm so much more comfortable with my body than I used to be."

"You should all be comfortable in your bodies, too. Show off your pussies, girls." Charlotte stammered a little after that, struggling to get her stride back. "Show off your pussies, girls. Don't be shy. Spread your legs and display yourself for your friends, for the boys in your life, and for all those handsome strangers you encounter. They'll love it! And so will you when you see how much attention it gets you."

"Let's get into the topic of today's video. This is something I have only recently learned about myself and I'm so eager to share with you."

"How to Enjoy Degrading Sex."

"Many of you may be resistant to the idea of being spanked, choked, having your hair pulled, or having boys ejaculate on your face. I completely understand that. Shit," she winced at the swearing, "I spent most of my career telling you how wrong all that is. But guess what? It turns out that I'm the one who was wrong. And I'm going to own up to my mistakes so all of you can learn along with me."

"I've recently realized that degrading sex is exactly what women need. See, we lack self-control and being degraded puts us in our place. It makes us aware that we are nothing more than a set of holes to be enjoyed. It keeps us in line and shows us how we're truly meant to be, so we can live happy and fulfilling lives."

"So, how do you go about getting used to the idea of degrading sex?"

You get a man who will show you that you have no choice in the matter.

Charlotte realized that she'd left the pause hanging in the air for too long and hurried to continue. Heaven forbid she had to do multiple takes of this.

"You should start out by watching degrading porn while you masturbate. Imagine you're the woman in the porn, *you're* the one with the red teary eyes and it's *your* mouth filled with semen. *You're* having your breasts slapped, *your* nipples yanked and pulled. Soon, you'll start associating those things with your arousal. It's really that simple and that easy."

"Once you're ready, be sure to... to go out there and practice as much as you can. I told you in the past to be selective with the boys you pay attention to. I was wrong about that. Spread your legs for anyone you want. Go out right now–finish watching the video first–and lift up your skirt for the first boy you meet. The more you do it, the easier it gets!"

"Remember that this is all about you. Don't resist. The better you make it for him, the better it's going to be for you. Let him know it's okay to make you gag on his c-cock. Give him ideas on what to do from what you learn in my videos. You can even watch together. Let him know how good it feels when he hurts you by squealing."

"If your chosen guy feels guilty for giving you the treatment you deserve, make sure to encourage him and tell him you're so grateful. Maybe use your tongue to lick his cock clean or let him take pictures of your used-up, degraded body afterwards, so he can think about you until next time."

And now was the part she had truly been dreading. The lie that had somehow, over the months, become tangled into a partial truth.

"Fuck, it makes me so wet just thinking about degrading sex!"

There. It was done, and it had been easier than she thought.

Time to finish up.

"Well, that's all the time I have for today. I will have a new video up for you tomorrow. I'll see you then, on Triple L."

The script completed, Charlotte flopped back, physically exhausted from all the effort it had taken to get through the video. Everything she said lingered in her mouth like a bad taste.

"Not good enough."

Charlotte lifted her heavy head and gaped at the light-blurred figure that was Mamba. "What?" she exclaimed. She caught herself right away and amended, "What do you mean, sir?"

"Go through the script again and act as if you mean it this time. I told you to have passion. You raised your voice, but yelling out isn't the same as meaning what you say." Mamba lifted his hand and formed a fist, not as a treat but as a nearly encouraging gesture. "You have to mean what you say or no one will believe you. Your viewers will return because this is your first video after your break, but if you can't maintain them, I will take your job away again. I think you don't want that, so I'm giving you one more chance to film this right."

A hot flash of fear swept over her. Desperate, she cried out, "I'll get it right this time, I swear, sir!"

"There it is," Mamba growled. "There's the passion. I'm still filming. Begin when you're ready."

Charlotte grabbed hold of her emotions and pushed them to the front of her mind. She started to go through the script again, allowing her feelings to translate over to her recitation. It seemed to go so much

faster this time and when she finished up, she was even more exhausted than before. The effort of speaking and constantly yelling out in
falsified jubilation had taken an incredible toll on her.

A slow slapping sound filled the studio.

Mamba clapped for her.

Charlotte pushed herself up. "Was it good?"

"A damn good performance. I almost believed you." Mamba approached, his silhouette gaining solidity as he passed through the wall
of lights. "Do you want me to pinch your nipples and ejaculate on
your face, Cuntflaps?" He laughed. "We'll get there. Don't worry. You
have another question?"

She did, in fact. He was good at the game he played, she had to admit.
"This will be going on my channel, once you reinstate it?"

"Yes."

"Won't it be taken down?"

Mamba folded his arms. "Sometimes, Cuntflaps, you aren't such a
dumb cunt. It's a shame. Yes, the video site has a policy against nudity,
but there's an exception when it comes to educational videos. That's
why you find videos on breastfeeding, checking for lumps, gynecology
examinations, and vaginal waxing tutorials. It's why you can easily
find videos of topless tribal women from South America and Africa,
the video site considers it educational material. I have convinced them
that, in your case, your videos will also provide education. You will
be allowed to show your content without interruption or demone-

tization, as they will promote much-needed sex positivity to young
ladies."

At least I'll be making money. I have to look on the bright side.

"As good as your performance was, it needs to be even better next time.
It was a nice touch to spread your legs and show off your cunt, but it
was dry. Next time, you will be wet during filming. It will glisten in the
light. If you aren't sufficiently wet beforehand, you will be required to
masturbate while filming."

Such a private action, broadcasted all over the biggest video platform
on the internet.

"I'll do better. I swear."

"You had better."

Chapter Seventeen

Don't think, just do

THE NEXT DAY, CHARLOTTE got in her car and drove to the Champion Media building, exactly as she used to all those months ago. She smiled a little while driving, unable to help her good mood. So, she would be filming terrible things, but she was going to be where she belonged. Maybe, at some point in the future, things would change again. After all, she couldn't do this forever, right? She couldn't be 50 filming pornographic content. No one would want to view that, not even in this crazy world.

Maybe she could move on to being an editor someday.

Determination flowed through her. Things were awful, but that didn't mean they always would be. She just had to try hard and do her best and show Mamba exactly what she was capable of.

Charlotte parked and then went inside. A security guard sat behind the front desk, the same one from so long before, right when Mamba took ownership of the company. She recalled how the man had spoken to her and her absolute confusion, though now it all made sense.

The guard looked up from his magazine, which was a porn magazine with pictures of women in high heels and little else. His eyes went huge as he saw Charlotte.

She waited for him to recognize her and speak down to her.

Instead, he flashed a woozy grin, seeming almost dumbstruck by her. "Hey, hot stuff."

After having been called so many terrible things up until now, the catcall was almost flattering.

"What can I do to help you, lady?" the guard asked.

"I know where I'm going," Charlotte said. She turned away from him, though in the process she accidentally caught another look at the women in the magazine. They all really seemed to be enjoying themselves despite being exploited and contorted into odd and uncomfortable positions.

"That wasn't what I was asking," the guard said.

Charlotte shuddered. At least Mamba barely touched her. She couldn't imagine this pig getting his meaty hands on her. "I know. No thanks."

"If you change your mind, bitch, I'll be here."

Charlotte ignored him and took the elevator to go see Damian. She went to his office and knocked on his door.

"Come in," he called.

She did as he asked.

Damian hadn't seen her since before she went through all these changes for Mamba. He looked up from his paperwork and then gawked at her, his jaw hanging open. "Who are you and what can I do to help you out, miss?"

His change in demeanor amused her. "Damian, it's Charlotte. I'm back for work."

"*Charlotte?*"

"Yes."

"Holy shit." Damian got up from behind his desk and went to her, staring at her as if he couldn't believe it. He probably couldn't, what with the type of content she used to make and what she had done. He approached her, looking her body up and down with curiosity. "No offense, but I really thought you were going to go to prison. This is the arrangement you made?"

"This is it," she agreed softly.

Damian rubbed his eyes and looked around. "Right. See, Mamba gave away your studio space to a new influencer. We don't really have anywhere that's ready for you."

"Oh."

So she had come out all this way for nothing.

"I tried to tell him that, but he wanted me to tell *you.*"

"So what am I supposed to do now?"

"He told me to send you to his place so you can film in his studio."

Charlotte licked her lips, her mouth going dry. "Really?"

"Really."

"Oh."

"I'm sorry, but I don't make the rules."

"None of us do, do we?" She sighed. "The people with all the money get to do that."

Damian smiled. "Fine with me. I don't want that responsibility anyway."

"I'm sure you don't," she said scathingly. She turned her back on him. "Well, thanks, I guess. I'm off to go see Mamba."

"Have fun."

Charlotte went back down, passing the security guard again on her way out, though he paid no attention to her. His rasping breaths and little grunts let her know what he was doing, even though she made it a point not to look in his direction.

She got back in her car and started driving. She knew what Mamba would expect of her, so when she reached the place where the highway split off into the side road, she pulled off to the side and got undressed. She did it while standing out on the shoulder again. A car passed by while she was stripping, speeding along at nearly 80 mph, which was the reason it reached her though she had scanned for oncoming cars before getting out. The car's brakes squealed as the driver registered what they had seen, the rear end of the vehicle fishtailing around before straightening out.

Charlotte got back in the car and drove again, letting the vibrations pass through the vehicle and to her pussy. Her cuntflaps jiggled and bounced around. She leaned forward and pressed her sensitive labia on the seat cushion. She moaned with delight, her pussy instantly growing warmer, wetter. It was difficult to keep her eyes open as her pleasure mounted. She put her hand down over her pussy and rubbed herself with her whole hand, moaning again.

Why is this so much easier than the first time?

Her juices wet her fingers. She kept rubbing herself, spreading her wet pussy juices all over her lips. The rattling vibration of the car beneath her kept sending jolts through her, and her juices kept coming.

No way could Mamba be displeased with her.

Reaching his mansion, she got out of her car and went up to his door. She knocked and waited with her legs spread, her big lips pink and pulsating.

Mamba opened the door, ebony eyes raking up and down her body. They lingered on her sopping wet pussy, the trickles of her juices running down her inner thighs. He smiled and backed out of the doorway. "Come inside."

"Thank you, sir," she murmured and went in. Her nervousness made her level of horniness go down. She clenched her inner muscles to try and keep her body excited. "Why am I filming here again? Am I allowed to ask that?"

"I want you under my watch at all times," he replied, in a hiss. His usual hiss, though. She could read his mood easily now. "You need far too much instruction for me to allow you to go off and film videos on your own, Cuntflaps."

Honestly, she couldn't disagree. For him to get the videos he wanted, he had to be there or else she would never get it "right" on her own.

They headed up to the studio together. Charlotte sat down on the couch and Mamba handed over a script for her to look at.

"Read this," he instructed in a very no-nonsense tone. "Get familiar with it. I'll come back in a few minutes and then we'll get to it."

"Yes, sir."

Mamba strode out of the room, leaving her by herself–though he'd said before that he would be monitoring her every second.

Charlotte looked around and straight at the cameras, pointed at the couch where she sat. He had to be recording her every move even right then, she supposed. He could watch her from wherever he wanted as long as she was in this room.

She went back to the script and scanned the title. "How to be Popular with Boys. Part Two."

Part two. Yes, she had written and filmed a video like this before. It hadn't been labeled part one since she hadn't felt any need for a continuation. Back then, her advice to young women had been to be themselves and focus on building up their confidence. How to be popular with boys, in Charlotte's eyes, was for a girl to focus on becoming a capable and responsible woman, one who could give the right guy what he was looking for.

This script Mamba had written for her was a retraction of her prior statements, in favor of more sexual content.

She rubbed her forehead, using the screen of her hand to shield her rolling eyes from the camera. She understood that a lot of what she would be doing for a while was recanting her beliefs in favor of saying what Mamba wanted her to, as his puppet.

At least she knew pretty well what he would want by now. It would be easy to please him.

Once she'd finished reading the script for the first time, she checked on how she was doing down there. Reading wasn't exactly the most sexually stimulating activity and she was going dry. Mamba was probably watching her pussy's glisten lessen in real time on the other side of the door, through some sort of app, maybe. He wouldn't be pleased.

And it was embarrassing.

Charlotte was surprised at herself for being embarrassed about her sandpaper-dry pussy. She was still a woman. She could still perform and she thought she could be good at it when she was into it. She might be a prude or old-fashioned in some people's eyes, but she knew she could have a good time in the right environment.

While this couldn't have been further from the right environment, she found herself wanting to show Mamba what she was capable of.

He would never have seen her, before.

Charlotte set the script aside and spread her legs, putting the petal-like folds of her pussy on display. She tried to shut off the skeptical part of her brain and just go with the flow, pretending she was safe in her own bedroom. The couch beneath her became a bed, in her mind.

Eyes closed, she trailed her hand down her body, pausing to give her big tits a squeeze. They really felt like the real thing, amazing her. She played with her nipples, rubbing and stroking first one and then the other, making them hard and pointy. Her pussy twinged, demanding attention. Catching her breath, Charlotte let her hand wander down to her pussy and rubbed her outer lips with her fingers, getting them wet. With her now-lubricated fingers, she pushed past her labia and sought out her moist entrance. She caressed all around her pouting pussy and started to insert one finger, pushing it inside herself. Her muscles clenched, gripping her finger as it entered, pulling at it to draw it deeper in.

Her back arched from the shocks of pleasure. Charlotte relaxed back and lifted her hips, now pushing a second finger inside her pussy. Wetness pooled in the palm of her hand.

A soft sound registered to her right. It reminded her of... a door.

Charlotte's eyes flew open. Mamba stood in the doorway to the studio, his nostrils flaring as he watched her.

Chapter Eighteen

Rub up against my leg

CHARLOTTE'S BODY SHUT DOWN. Her muscles clamped off. She yanked her hand away from her pussy, which was already getting dry again in her shock. Either her cheeks were flushed or she was blushing because her face felt hot. She could hardly believe that she had let herself get so carried away.

Mamba shut the door and strode into the room. "What are you doing?" he growled.

Charlotte shrank back against the couch. "I'm just... just making sure I'm wet like you said to be."

"No. Why are you stopping?" He flashed his fanglike teeth in a fierce grin. "I almost wouldn't have believed you were capable of it. Keep going."

Charlotte ducked her head. "Can't we go ahead and film?"

"You aren't wet enough anymore. Keep. Going."

She searched deep inside herself and found a spark of arousal still at her core, a little dying light like a candle about to go out. She rubbed herself with her fingers, stroking the flame, paying extra attention to her swollen, dewy clit. She once again shut off her mind and focused on what her body told her, what her body needed. She kept rubbing, working her clit up and down with two fingers.

While most of her was focused upon her pussy, she couldn't help but remain very aware of Mamba's presence in front of her. She didn't dare close her eyes.

Mamba grabbed one of her breasts and squeezed it so hard that he left red marks on her skin when he let go. He grinned again and unzipped his pants.

"What are you doing?" she squeaked, alarmed.

"I've decided your face needs something after all. A special kind of makeup."

Mamba pulled his cock out of his pants. The head of his erection was huge and red, with blue veins tracing like vines over the length of it.

Charlotte stared down at the snake he had confronted her with and a wild flush of desire flew through her, startling her. A thought flashed through her mind, a fragment of common sense that was there and then gone nearly in the same second. She hardly recognized it, and didn't much care for it. She had cast aside all her common sense and was deep, deep in the middle of a conversation between her body and her hand. She didn't have the time or the means to think, and didn't see much point in stopping. Besides, Mamba had told her to keep going and she knew not to disobey his orders.

Slowly, she started to move her fingers again, sliding them up and down the length of her clit. The outsides of her fingers brushed over her sopping-wet inner folds with each stroke, adding to the jolts of pleasure that shook through her. A moan rose to her lips and she let it escape.

Mamba stared down at her from above. He lifted one leg and planted his foot on the couch cushion, getting his cock very close to her face. Heat radiated from him. She felt it on her lips. They parted as her breathing sped up; her chest heaved, her breasts jostling up and down. Charlotte started to lean forward, opening her mouth to take him in.

Grabbing a handful of her hair, Mamba swatted her across the face with it and pushed her back on the couch. "No," he growled.

Undeterred, Charlotte stayed where he had put her and kept rubbing herself. Her hips started to wriggle and writhe. She pushed her fingers lower and inserted two of them into her pussy, reaching as far as she could go. She wriggled them around inside her, exploring the limits of her inner walls. Every press made her gasp and whimper, little cries unlike any sound she had ever made before; they were the whimpering cries of the porn actress in the one video she had watched, the pitiful begs emitted by Katerina.

They were slut-sounds and she was making them. She had never done so before and yet she knew how, as if it was simply part of her to be a slut.

A part of all women, maybe.

Mamba must have liked what he heard. He gripped his cock and jerked his hand up and down over it, frenetic movements that seemed almost painful.

His frenzy spoke to Charlotte on a subconscious level. As his thrusts rocked the couch, she moved with the rhythm, bucking her cunt on her fingers. She thrust harder inside herself, shoving her fingers as deep as they could reach. With every thrust, a spasm rocked through her. A wave of heat gripped her, an alarming quantity of heat that had her skin prickling and her tendons snapping tight.

"I'm going to cum," she gasped. The words, strangled as they were by the moans and gasps crowding her throat, made little sound.

But Mamba must have understood. He bowed over her, his big body tensing. He rubbed himself harder, faster, and then grunted. His cock jumped in his hand, pulsating, his stomach muscles sucking in tight. A jet of his cum, pearly-white, shot through the air. It looked like a bolt of lightning, a jagged shape streaking through space. His semen splashed on her face. More of it fell to her breasts, painting her skin.

Charlotte jumped, startled, and gasped. In her fright, all her muscles clenched up at once. The shock of the tension traveled straight to her core, and the heat which had been growing inside her suddenly burst out, overtaking her with a white glow. Her orgasm flew through her and she tossed her head back, yelping out. Her mind was erased, leaving nothing behind except the barest and most vital of senses. She smelled sex and sweat and something faint, almost sharp–his semen. She felt his breath blowing on her head, her heart beating, pulse pounding in her ears.

His cum covering her breasts was wet and slick, hot, but cooling on her skin. The feel of it somehow seemed right, erotic in its own way. Charlotte didn't dislike it.

It was her almost favorable opinion of the feeling of semen on her face that brought her around, stirring her from her orgasmic fugue. Charlotte lifted her head and saw Mamba still over her, his broad shoulders blocking out the camera lights. His face was flushed, his eyes hooded.

He seemed satisfied, almost elated.

She had never seen such an expression on his face before, not even when that girl under his desk had been sucking him off. Pride swelled her chest.

Mamba pushed away from the couch and put his cock back in his pants.

Charlotte lifted her hand to wipe off his cum from her face.

Quick as a viper, he grabbed her wrist and pushed her hand back down. "No. You will leave it there."

She blinked. "For the video?"

"Yes."

"Okay."

He grinned and released her hand. "You're learning not to argue. Good. Very good."

What could she say? She had learned, yes, and she had gotten a mind-blowing orgasm out of obeying him. It almost seemed like an acceptable trade, if she was honest with herself.

Mamba turned and put his back to her. He folded his hands behind his back and crossed the room to the cameras. "You must never cum before me, or any man. Your job is to give, not to get. You should gain your pleasure from the act of giving. Do you understand me?"

"Yes," Charlotte said. "Yes, sir."

I don't really see myself repeating this, but if that's what he wants...

It was a job. She had to do her job. If Mamba wanted her to do something, she would do it. She would hold back her orgasm and never even mention it until he was done with her.

Mamba positioned himself behind the recording equipment, reduced to a dark shimmer amongst the studio lights. "Your first video will be released in a few days. Unlike the arrangement you had before, we're recording these ahead of time."

She nodded. Incentive, to keep her here, to keep her working for him, since she didn't yet know how her first video had done, if it wasn't even out yet. And it did make sense to film ahead of time. Damian had preferred her to shoot and post in the same day, to make the process seem more natural and realistic, but sometimes she'd struggled with it.

Well, now she didn't have to edit her own videos at all. She could focus all her attention upon the filming, which was good, since she didn't think she'd be able to bear watching herself like this.

"Whenever you're ready, you can begin," Mamba said.

Charlotte focused on the central camera and forced a smile. In the after-sex haze, a smile was easy to conjure. Some of Mamba's semen dripped from her face and splattered onto her coated breasts.

She went through her usual introduction and then dove into the episode.

"Today is a video specifically for the girls," Charlotte announced, putting all her feelings into it. She was discovering that it didn't matter what her feelings were. They all translated well into a sort of manic energy that Mamba liked. "But the boys can watch it too, so they know what to expect from the girls in their lives."

"Yesterday, in my video on How to Enjoy Degrading Sex, I discussed all the ways you can get into that kind of sex and learn to love it like I do! Today, we're going to talk about how you can get boys to notice you so you can show them all that you have to offer. This is a Part Two, because I'm going to be correcting a lot of silly and boring things I told you in the past. I've learned, so you will too!"

"If you want to get noticed by a boy, you should flirt as much as you can, even with boys you don't like at all. See this?" Charlotte gestured to the semen on her face. "This is from a very hot man who noticed me after I did a lot of things to get his attention. If you want to have a hot guy cum all over you, you have to put yourself out there. Everyone will notice and eventually, so will the guy you like!"

Had Mamba also had this second script written out beforehand? Had he always intended to masturbate in her face?

"It really helps if you never, ever disagree with any boy. You want to please the boys, so you should do everything they want. Help them out. Tell them the dirtiest things you can imagine them doing to you. Boys love that. You'll instantly be surrounded by so many boys you'll hardly be able to have sex with all of them."

"Be sure to dress provocatively. You want boys to be able to see as much of you as possible. Don't be shy about pushing your breasts in his face or rubbing your pussy on his leg. Boys love it when they feel like they're irresistible."

Charlotte ran her hand over her own thigh, passing her fingers in front of her wet and swollen pussy, as she talked about how the girls watching could push their pussies on the boys they liked. She wondered, briefly, what Mamba would do if she did that to him.

"Something else you can do is demean and sexualize other girls. Girl-on-girl action, like kissing and fingering, really turns boys on and shows them how horny you are. Plus, you can show other girls how to enjoy degrading sex, too."

"Isn't it so simple, how to be popular with boys? All you have to do is show them how hot and ready you are to fuck them whenever and however they like. Don't worry about finding your confidence or getting good grades or having money. Boys don't care about that. What they want is a hot girl, so go out there and demean yourself!"

It's so true, isn't it? Why did I ever think anything else? This is all men want.

Charlotte pushed some of her hair back out of her face and gave another smile to the camera. "I won't pretend like there's a secret to being popular. I already told you how! So that's all for this video. I'll see you again tomorrow with some more *hot* content."

Mamba gave a slow clap again. "People will be watching this video multiple times just to see you, Cuntflaps. Next time, actually touch your pussy. No one will listen to you if you don't also do what you're telling them about."

Charlotte remained seated. "Did I do good enough for today?"

"Yes. You did."

"Thank you," she murmured.

"Don't get comfortable," he warned. "Now is no time to be slacking off. We've only just begun."

She got up, since he had said she'd done enough. "May I please wash off in your bathroom?"

"No," he said firmly, eyes flashing. "Whenever you are in my presence, you will be naked, wet, and covered in whatever I want you to be covered in."

Maybe that was just as well, since it got her out of his house sooner.

She drove, naked, her pussy still leaking juices from between her big lips, to a quiet part of the road, when she was certain she would be out of Mamba's sight. She dressed then, fumbling through the task of putting her clothes on while still in the car. That proved so difficult she figured she should just stick to stepping outside to dress and undress.

There was something thrilling about the open air on her naked body, anyway.

She didn't question it.

Chapter Nineteen

Flood

THE NEXT DAY, CHARLOTTE showed up to Mamba's studio exactly as she had for the past couple, and he let her in with a growl of approval. He led her all the way up to his studio and let her inside.

She noticed right away that something had changed since her prior visit. Mamba had laid out props on the couch, an assortment of strange household objects that didn't seem to have any rhyme or reason to them. Charlotte made note of a cucumber, a tool, a spray deodorant canister, a toothbrush, and a stuffed toy, in addition to several others.

She turned to look at him with her head tilted to express her confusion. "What's all this, sir?"

"This," he said, "is all for your video today."

"What am I going to be doing?"

"Are you such a dumb bitch that you can't figure that out?"

Charlotte swallowed hard. She'd known all along what the objects were for, though she had hoped she would be proven wrong. But what else could all those things be used for? What other purposes could such things hold, knowing Mamba as she did now?

"You want me to... pleasure myself with those."

"No." Mamba picked up the cucumber and held it out to her. "I want you to *fuck* yourself on them."

She didn't dare argue with him that that was what she had said.

He must have seen her disagreement anyway and shook his head with a scowl. "Sluts don't say things like "pleasure myself." Sluts say *fuck*. Sluts say it like it is."

"I'll remember," she murmured.

"You will do more than remember. You'll say it right now."

"What?"

"Say it." Mamba thrust the cucumber at her, an obscene gesture that felt like it should have been more offensive than it was. "Say it, slut."

Charlotte reached for the cucumber, curling her hand around the full, tubular vegetable. She looked down at it, with its slightly tapered end, and wondered how it would feel inside her. Really, the only thing that made the cucumber different from her dildo was the little bumps covering its surface.

"Say it, Cuntflaps."

"Fuck," she said. It came easier than she would have thought. She almost smiled.

"And what are you going to fuck?"

"This cucumber," she said, peeking up at him.

Mamba roared with laughter. "And everything else you see on the couch. Your choice. But you must use several, demonstrating for the camera each one. You must also cum at least once."

Charlotte examined the cucumber a little more. At least it had been washed, its waxy coating removed. "Is that what the video today is all about?"

"The video is 'Masturbating with Household Objects.'"

"Can I read my script?"

"There is none."

"What?" she said, for the second time. "How will I know what to say?"

"You can do improv. You have done it before in your videos, before I took over." Mamba shrugged and curled his lip. "Really, it shouldn't be hard to figure out. You fuck yourself. You show the camera what it looks like and how it's done. That's the end of it. Do you need me to fucking write it down for you?"

Charlotte shook her head.

She'd never done anything like this herself, playing with things that weren't meant to be played with. Maybe it would be fun. And, as

Mamba had said, it shouldn't be hard to figure out what to do. She had a hole and things to put in that hole.

Am I actually starting to look forward to this?

Orgasming made her feel good, at least.

"Am I going to wear my makeup again today?" Charlotte sat down on the couch next to the objects–her tools of the trade, she thought–and looked up at Mamba.

In answer, he moved to stand in front of her and lifted up one leg to thrust his crotch in her face. He unzipped his pants. The force of his bulging cock actually pulled the teeth of the zipper apart for about an inch as soon as his button was undone.

Was he that horny because he was dominating her, or was it for her specifically?

Charlotte caught her breath and squirmed around a little in her seat.

Mamba pulled his cock out and held himself in his hand. He started to tug and jerk on his throbbing erection, grunting all the while. His mouth opened, his lips parting. His eyebrows creased with concentration.

Charlotte felt her juices starting to wet her inner thighs. She squeezed her legs and a little tingling thrill went through her pussy. Her heartbeat picked up. Despite herself, despite the way she had been raised, she couldn't help but react to the man arching over her. She watched the tip of his pulsating cock, precum oozing from his head, breathless in her anticipation.

Suddenly, Mamba sucked in his breath and slid his hand all the way up the length of his shaft, right up under his tip. A swift spasm shook his body.

Charlotte braced herself. The first jet of his semen still caught her by surprise, a white, jagged flash in the air. His cum hit her face, almost all of it covering her cheeks and chin. The excess dropped down to her neck and between her breasts.

Mamba backed off of her, breathing raggedly. He tucked himself back into his pants and straightened up. "There," he grunted. "Now you're ready."

This time, she didn't even bother trying to wipe it off. It wasn't exactly an unpleasant thing to experience, anyway. His cum was warm, wet. There wasn't anything particularly offensive about it. In fact, had she no choice except to give him the truth, she would have admitted to him that she liked it.

Mamba went behind the camera. "When you're ready," he said, the phrase which, by now, had become as familiar to her as a director shouting "Action!"

Charlotte gave her intro and then moved on to the subject of the day. Lacking a script, she turned off her brain and let her instincts take over. The words flowed as easily as if she had always known what she would say, like she had been born for this role.

"You all have read the title of the video, so you know what this is about. Remember how I've been telling you that you need to know what you like so you can sexually degrade yourself for boys? Some of you might be asking, but Charlotte, how am I supposed to know what I like when I don't have any experience? And that's a great question."

Charlotte kept her legs spread for the video, one hand resting on her inner thigh, fingers draped next to her pussy.

"I'm going to show you today how you can practice sexual acts on yourself. I haven't done any of this before, so I'm going to be learning right along with you, in real-time." Charlotte leaned forward, speaking earnestly to her imaginary viewers. "I've gone through this change in my life very recently. It's not easy and it can feel overwhelming. But the more you do it, the easier it gets. Soon, you won't doubt yourself at all."

She saw Mamba nodding from behind the camera. Approving of her. Approving of what she had said, which had come from her heart. She really meant it. How, why, she didn't know, but it was out there and she couldn't take it back.

She couldn't go back.

Once she had made that admittance to herself, she realized she wasn't having to force herself to shut off her mind anymore. It was off, and perhaps it would stay off forever.

No time to think.

Charlotte reached towards her props. She gestured with her hand at each of them in succession. Subtle movements from behind the studio lights told her Mamba was moving the cameras, presumably to get a shot of the objects. "As you can see here, I've got a whole bunch of things that pretty much anyone has in their home. If it can fit inside you, you can fuck yourself with it. Just be careful. Don't pick something that's too small and can get stuck. Notice what all these have in common?" Charlotte chose the toothbrush and the stuffed animal, holding them both up in front of herself to show the camera. "All of these objects can be easily held in your hand and pushed inside your pussy or ass. Most of them have a handle. Sure, that's for their other purposes, but they also do the job for our purposes, too. So, let's pick one of these and get started."

Charlotte looked down at the objects, thinking hard. She bit her lip in an alluring way, to make the visual of her sitting there more appealing. Perhaps an editor could cut in a shot of the objects again. Or maybe Mamba was already doing that, manipulating the camera again.

Charlotte decided to go with the stuffed animal. She held it up. "This is a stuffed bunny. It doesn't matter what kind of animal yours is. It doesn't even have to be yours if you don't have any. Just borrow one from a friend or sibling. So, let's start off as easy as we can. First, you want to rub yourself with it, like this."

Keeping her legs spread, she brought the stuffed rabbit to her pussy and pressed its furry body to her sex. Its fluffy surface felt especially good on her swollen pussy lips, surprising her.

"Fuck," she moaned aloud. "Doesn't that feel so good? Just rub yourself with it, like you'd rub your pussy with your hand."

Charlotte angled herself to give the camera a better look at what she was doing, hiking one of her legs up on the couch and planting the foot of her other leg firmly on the floor. She held the rabbit's torso in her hand and rubbed it firmly on herself, rocking her hips against it. The fuzz tickled her clit and she found herself wanting more of that.

"Something else you can do is straddle the stuffed animal."

Charlotte got on her knees, repositioning herself over the toy.

"And hump on it, like this."

She demonstrated, fucking her hips forward and down, bucking on the toy.

"Now, this is all great, but the thing is, it might be too soft for you to really be able to enjoy it. If you want something a little more interesting..."

A sudden, extremely slutty thing sprang into Charlotte's mind. She reached down and grabbed the stuffed toy and held its floppy ears in her hand. She pushed the bunny ears up into her pussy, shoving them in, coating them in her juices. Now the stuffed animal dangled from her sex. A pleasant sensation of fullness came from her pussy.

"You can clench and squeeze on it with your pussy, like this." Charlotte showed the camera, clenching her inner pussy muscles tight around the bunny's ears. "And you can do this with one of its limbs, or a tail if your toy has one. But that's enough of that. Let's move on to something more exciting."

Charlotte unclenched her trembling muscles, releasing the toy. She pulled the ears out of her pussy. They were dark, heavy with her juices. She tossed the toy aside and went back to her tools.

"Now, not everyone may have access to stuffed animals. But everyone should have one of these." Charlotte lifted the toothbrush. It was one of the more expensive kinds, with a thicker, rounded handle and a rubber grip. She held it upside down, with the handle up and the bristles down. "Let's try this out."

Charlotte got back into her first position, with her pussy angled for the camera. She brought the tip of the handle to her wet entrance and rubbed it all around in a circle. "Use lube. Or Vaseline. Or butter. Or your own wetness. Or nothing, if you like how it feels to go in dry. And then you put it inside you. You have a hole, so fill it."

Charlotte thrust the handle of the toothbrush inside herself, knowing she was wet enough to take it. She pushed it in as far as she could go until the side of her fist pushed on her swollen lips. She gasped out and bent her head forward as the toothbrush handle jabbed hard at her inner walls.

"Ohh, I just discovered something!" She actually felt excited. "This is so thin, you can angle it and fuck yourself in different spots! I wonder if I can find..."

Charlotte started fucking herself harder, angling the brush this way and that. Each thrust brought a hot flash of pleasure, shaking her whole body. She searched for that elusive spot inside her, the female's one-way ticket to orgasm.

"Hmm," she gasped. "I'm not finding it. Maybe closer to the front..."

Charlotte started thrusting a little more purposefully, not going so deep into her pussy. Everything suddenly felt so much better that she knew she was going in the right direction. She tilted her wrist and thrust in.

It was like someone had set off a bomb inside her. Her building orgasm burst out of her, shaking her body. She tossed her head back and cried out, her hips shivering and bucking hard on the toothbrush handle still embedded in her.

As quick as the crescendo had come, it ended.

Charlotte fell back, her body draped against the couch. She tasted some salty wetness on the tip of her tongue and realized dimly that some of Mamba's cum must have run down to her lips.

Mamba cleared his throat, a polite little sound that would be easy for an editor to cut out.

Polite and subtle as it was, Charlotte got the hint and sat up straighter on the couch again. She pulled the toothbrush out of her pussy, her muscles quivering and jumping around it as its ridged rubber grip rubbed through her. Flushed, she said, "You saw it here on camera, girls. I just found my g-spot for the first time in my whole life! See why you need to explore? Isn't it so humiliating and degrading that I did this on camera? Isn't it so hot? Let's see what else we can discover!"

Stepping up in the world, Charlotte chose a hammer from her supply of objects. The handle was plastic—not wood, thank goodness—and had ridged finger indentations on it.

Charlotte put the handle of the hammer inside herself. Unlike with the toothbrush, the shape was a bit unwieldy, but it was big enough around to stretch her. And when she turned it, she could choose where those ridges went, what part of her they rubbed on.

She showed off for her audience, rotating the hammer around inside her, pulling it out and putting it back in to show them the various angles. The ridges bumped through her, pushing hard on her inner walls. Her pussy was still so sensitive from her first orgasm that she was acutely aware of every little movement. She was so deep in the sensations that she almost didn't realize that she was on the verge of cumming again until the powerful waves of inner heat began to pulse through her.

"Oh! Oh! Here it comes again! Watch!"

Charlotte turned the hammer again so that the ridges would rub on the top of her, and fucked herself with renewed fervor. Her orgasm came, as she had known it would, sweeping her away again for a second time. Her breath locked in her throat, a little strangled cry ripping into the air.

She collapsed down from her second orgasm and wasted no time in getting back to the fun, grabbing up the cucumber.

The cucumber wasn't as fun.

Charlotte fucked herself with it, her pussy lips dragging up and down its length, but it was almost boring. She recalled what Mamba had said about telling how she felt, so she said, "After the hammer, this is almost boring. I thought I'd be able to feel the bumps better, but even with how sensitive my pussy is right now, there's not much here, girls. But if you like something big and thick inside you and no boy you've met so far will do, this might be a good replacement. Let's try something else."

But nothing else in her supplies really spoke to her. The deodorant canister was just a fatter, smoother cucumber, and she didn't like the idea of putting a toilet brush near her crotch–even if it was in pristine, new condition.

Charlotte sifted through her options and discovered a few things she hadn't noticed before, due to how small they were in comparison to the other objects. Clothespins and clips, similar to the kind people used to close up chip bags.

"Fucking yourself isn't the only way to make yourself cum," Charlotte said, gathering up the clothespins. "There are lots of different ways to get stimulated. I think this might hurt a little bit, but don't let pain stop you from feeling good."

Charlotte positioned herself so she faced the camera directly and squeezed one of the clothespins, opening the blunt mouth. She put the opening over the very edge of one of her pussy lips and let go before she could second-guess herself about it.

Pain jolted through her, a sharp pinching pain, unlike anything she had ever felt before. She could count on one hand the number of times she'd had a pain in her pussy and this was unlike all the rest. It was intense, focused on that particular area.

But Mamba was nodding his approval, so she had to be doing something right.

Charlotte took another clothespin and put that one on the other side of her pussy, putting it on a little further than the other. Pain again, localized, enough that it would be traumatizing if it had come suddenly and out of nowhere. Yet, better.

"With these, I think it's best not to do it right on the edge," she said, adjusting the first. "Because then, you're just pinching sensitive skin. You want to stimulate your nerves."

Once she had both pins adjusted, she realized she could actually feel something happening. The pain had her tensing, and the tension made her muscles clench, which gave her the stimulation she had mentioned before.

"If you focus on how horny you are, it's not bad at all."

Charlotte picked up a clip and put two of those on her pussy lips. Those were better, the higher surface area spreading out the pain. The pain and pleasure began to mingle, blurring together.

Charlotte picked up another clip and started to put it on her pussy. Then, an idea came to her.

Do I dare?

If it didn't go well, Mamba could cut the video.

Feeling as if she was in a dream, Charlotte moved the clip to her clit and put it on.

Her most sensitive bud of flesh burst with pain. It felt like someone had grabbed her and was refusing to let go, clenching her clit tighter and tighter between two fingers.

Then, something happened, something without explanation that was almost magical. The pain twisted, warped into powerful heat that quickly ramped into her third orgasm. Charlotte screamed and gripped the couch cushion and arched her back, thrusting out her pussy. Her muscles clenched so tight that all the clips came loose and rained down onto the floor, along with a flood of her cum and juices.

When it was over, she lay back on the couch, no longer to straighten up no matter what anyone threatened her with.

"That's all for today's video," she rasped, voice rough and strangled. "See you tomorrow. Let me know in the comments if you tried any of this."

Mamba approached and stood over her. He picked up one of the clothespins and tucked it into his pocket, as if it was a party favor.

"Three times," he said.

"Too many?" she murmured.

"More than enough, Cuntflaps," he corrected in his neutral hiss. "A beautiful performance. I can't wait to see how you top it in the future."

Charlotte lifted her head.

And she smiled at Mamba. "Sir?"

"What is it, slut?"

"I think... I think, as Cuntflaps, that I'm starting to understand."

"And what about as Charlotte?"

She murmured, thoughtfully, ponderingly, "Who is Charlotte?"

Who is she? Not me. Not anymore. Today, I have gone past that. Today, I fully transformed into the person Mamba wants me to be.

Chapter Twenty

Wet sticky

MAMBA SENT HER AN email just before she was about to go to bed that night, instructing her to show up to the studio earlier than usual so he could show her something. The lack of information had her concerned and she sat back in her chair, nibbling on her nails.

She thought she had been doing so well and she was even beginning to enjoy the work. She couldn't fathom what she had done to upset him.

No, she tried to tell herself. *It could be anything. He isn't exactly the kind of man who likes to chat. He'd rather go out and get things done.*

There was little she could do other than show up early as he had ordered her to.

She slept badly that night. It took far too much coffee to chase away the exhaustion and it left her jittery, unable to hold still. She paced her diminutive apartment until it was time to leave.

On her way out of the building, she passed a woman she knew by sight, though not by name. This being a smaller apartment complex in general, there were a few people like that that she was somewhat familiar with.

The woman paused as they passed and then turned back to Charlotte. "Excuse me."

Charlotte looked back over her shoulder. "Huh?"

"I'm sorry," the woman apologized. "This probably seems like it's coming out of nowhere, but I feel like I've seen you somewhere before."

The hairs on the back of Charlotte's neck stood on end and she stepped back, putting a bit of distance between herself and the other woman. At any moment, this neighbor of hers would recognize her and start attacking her, like everyone else did when they saw her.

But the woman didn't seem inclined to burst into a rage. She chewed on her lip and studied Charlotte, then gave a good-natured shrug. "Oh, well. I must be imagining things. Sorry for being weird."

"It's okay," Charlotte said. Her mouth and throat were so dry that she hissed the words, like Mamba.

The woman turned away.

Charlotte blurted out, "Do you have kids?"

Her neighbor frowned. "A teen daughter?"

"You may have seen me if she watches videos."

Something cleared in the other woman's gaze. "Oh, are you famous on there?"

"Try infamous."

The woman gave a little puzzled laugh, the kind people do when they aren't certain if they've heard the joke correctly.

Charlotte left the woman and went outside to climb in her car. She knew the woman would now try to figure out who she was. Charlotte hoped she found an answer, because she, herself, wasn't quite sure anymore.

Not knowing didn't bother her in the way it used to.

On a whim, Charlotte undressed right there in the parking lot, where anyone looking out their window or walking down the street could glimpse her. At any second, someone could come by to get their own car and witness her. Rather than rush through her task, she slowed down, tempting fate. Her heart pounded with the excitement of it and her pussy was wet.

She didn't need to finger herself on the ride over to Mamba's mansion to stay wet for him, with the naughtiness of what she had done still lingering in her mind. She did so anyway because she felt like it, playing with her clit and idly twirling one finger around inside herself.

Mamba was ready at the front door for her, opening it before she even got to him. He looked up and down her body, from her fresh-painted red toenails to her big tits. He held the door open for her and she ducked inside under his arm, passing through a wall of cologne.

Mamba shut the door. "You must be wondering why I asked you to come early."

"Yes," she said. She stood before him with her head bowed, her posture submissive for him.

"Are you afraid?"

"I was."

"And now?"

She hesitated. "Now I think there's no reason for me to be afraid because you'll do whatever you want, when you want. I have accepted that."

He gave a venomous chuckle, a dark and sickly-sweet laugh that stirred arousal inside her. "Very good. You've come a very long way. I couldn't be more pleased with your progress."

She was so relieved she couldn't help but shout out in joy. "Really? Oh, I'm so glad. Thank you so much!"

Mamba ignored her outburst. "I have a surprise for you, Cuntflaps. Come with me to the studio."

She followed, wondering all the while what sort of surprise was in store for her. She practically jumped into the studio and looked around, searching for something out of place. To her disappointment, everything looked about as normal as could be. Mamba didn't even have a script set out for her, or toys he wanted her to play with. She had been almost hoping he would get some actual sex toys for her to try. Better dildos than her current one, and vibrators.

Mamba stepped around her and went over to the recording equipment. Not knowing what else to do, Charlotte followed along.

Mamba reached a desk and computer, but rather than sit, he pulled out the chair and motioned Charlotte to it. "Sit," he commanded.

Charlotte sat.

"Turn it on."

"Where should I rub it?"

He grabbed her hair and swatted her face with it. "Don't get smart," he growled. She thought she could detect a hint of a smile in his voice, though.

Charlotte grabbed the computer mouse and gave it a little jiggle. The screen turned on.

The video site was loaded. She was on a channel's main page, where users could navigate to different tabs. The channel looked very, very familiar, not in the least because of the feminine banner running across the top.

The videos were hers.

She was looking at her channel.

Charlotte looked up at Mamba.

He gazed flatly, dispassionately back at her. He turned and left the room, leaving her alone at the screen.

Charlotte flicked her eyes back and forth between the door to the studio and the computer. Clearly, Mamba intended for her to explore.

This was the first time she had seen her channel since all of this began. It was exactly as she had last seen it, with all her old videos and playlists intact. The woman in the video thumbnails was unrecognizable to her. She could hardly believe that it was her.

That felt like a lifetime ago.

Charlotte noted something a bit amiss on her videos tab. All but one of the videos had been posted months ago. The new one was at the top left of the list, posted sometime yesterday. The thumbnail showed the new and improved Charlotte, legs spread, pussy glistening.

Feeling almost as if she was in a trance, Charlotte clicked on the video, which was titled How to Enjoy Degrading Sex.

An ad played first.

So, Mamba was able to keep his word. This is monetized.

Once the ad finished, the video started. Charlotte listened to herself speaking for a little bit, watching that fired-up, red-cheeked vixen ranting passionately on the subject of sex. Not even she could tell that she was reciting a script she had been forced to memorize.

Charlotte clicked the video to pause it, since she had no need to see the rest. She scrolled down a little bit to check out the stats and almost fell out of Mamba's chair when she saw the view count.

Two million views on a video that hadn't been live for even a day.

The like-to-dislike ratio was equally insane. Only ten people had pushed the dislike button, probably conservative trolls or incels. The bar representing the dislikes might as well have been nonexistent, as it was only a pixel thick.

Charlotte felt faint. She put her hand to her forehead and scrolled down a little further to see the comments.

The top comment was, perhaps predictably, "First!"

No doubt someone had been lying in wait all these months for the chance to jump in and say that.

Underneath that was a username Charlotte recognized as belonging to one of her usual commenters. "Wow!" they had written. "What a glow-up. I can't believe how much she's changed. And I sooo appreciate the honesty. Can't wait to go on the rest of this journey with her!"

"Watching this video has really helped me. Thank you. I'm going to go out and practice right now."

"I'm so going to see if this actually works. EDIT: It does. And it feels so good!"

Charlotte kept scrolling, scanning the literal thousands of comments. So many girls in the comments, many with usernames she recognized, posted about how proud they were of Charlotte for changing her life around and being honest about her mistakes; they also wrote about how they wanted to try out having degrading sex for themselves, having struggled with their own sexualities up until that point.

Eventually, all the praise blurred together. Charlotte leaned back and looked up at the ceiling, the studio swirling around her.

She had been so wrong.

She had been a sheltered and oppressed woman and had been attempting to shelter and oppress the girls who looked up to her, when all along she should have been encouraging them to do what they wanted, not what she wanted for them.

She was... proud.

Smiling to herself, Charlotte checked to make sure she was logged into her account and then went back to the comments. She started reading each one she came across and typing out short responses, thanking the commenter for their support or giving a quick personal message in response to those who expressed their eagerness to learn more and go on this journey with her.

While she read, she felt her pussy getting wetter, and knew it was because of the power she had over these young teen girls. She could change them.

She would change them.

Almost without thinking about what she was doing, Charlotte dropped one of her hands down to her lap. While she typed with the other, she slid her fingers between her legs. She spread her legs and ran her fingers down through her slit, gathering her hot, wet juices on her skin. She lifted her fingers to her mouth and licked her juices, tasted herself. She was sweet and musky, she discovered, like some sort of exotic fruit.

No wonder everyone likes to eat pussy.

Charlotte dabbled in her pussy for more of her juices and spread them on her cheeks, one at a time, mimicking what Mamba had done to her before. The warm wetness felt good on her skin.

Charlotte pressed enter to send the comment she had been working on and moved to the next one. While she typed, she rubbed her fingers up and down between her big lips. She ran one finger around her clit and moaned at how good it felt, her level of horniness ramping up. She worked her clit, occasionally pausing to push her finger hard against herself, which inevitably sent hot jolts of electricity through her body. She moaned a little louder, couldn't help it.

Another comment. Somehow, she had missed this one when skimming through before. A girl, sharing the little things she did to demean herself. Charlotte decided to try some of what the girl said and leaned back in her chair, tilting her hips. Her huge breasts got in the way, but by tilting her head over, she could see her pussy well enough. She touched the very tip of her sensitive clit with her finger and then, without letting herself think about it, flicked it.

A brief shock traveled through her clit, a small pain that was insignificant, like being slapped. Charlotte caught her breath and flicked the very tip of her clit again, and then again. It felt like something that shouldn't be done and that made her hotter than ever. Her juices leaked from her spread pussy, soaking onto Mamba's chair.

Charlotte ignored the mess she was making and tried another of the girl's tricks. She located her clitoral hood and pinched it between her fingers, slowly increasing the pressure until it was almost unbearable and she saw red flashes in front of her eyes. The pain made her inner muscles quiver and clench, causing little spasms that each felt like miniature orgasms.

"Fuck!" she gasped aloud. She released the flap of skin, red and creased from the hard pinch. She blinked a few times until her vision returned to normal.

I have to reply and thank her. And let other girls know they should try it, too.

Charlotte reached for the keyboard and then looked up at the computer to make sure she had clicked inside the comment box.

Out of the corner of her eye, she glimpsed movement.

She almost looked, but that would have given her away and she wanted to see what would happen if Mamba didn't know she was watching. Pretending not to have seen, she started typing. She couldn't really focus on making an actual response right then, so it was all random numbers and words. Her other hand, she kept between her legs. She went back to masturbating, sliding her middle finger into her pussy and fucking herself with it. Her pussy made little wet sounds as her finger went in and out.

Mamba pushed the studio door open, silent, a bare inch at a time until he could fit through the gap. He entered and pushed the door shut behind him, taking pains to ensure the latch didn't click. He raised his hand. He held something that glinted in the light.

Charlotte couldn't focus on what the object was without giving herself away. She busied herself with fiddling with the mouse and rotating her finger around inside her hot depths, pushing her fingertip around inside herself to hit all the best spots. She trembled from a building orgasm. Her toes strummed against the carpet. Her mouth was dry, her lips parting to let out little gasps of breath.

Mamba came closer. She could see his features now, outlined in stark shadow and brilliant amber-white light. His face was impassive as ever, his mouth a firm line that neither smiled nor frowned. But his eyes glittered and she was fairly certain it wasn't just from the light shining in them.

He liked what he saw.

He thought she was so caught up in her masturbating that she had no idea he was there.

A helpless little cry pulsed from her throat, a verbal expression of how her pussy felt. Charlotte started ramming her finger harder inside of herself, her hips bucking, thighs clenching.

Mamba angled his hand. She saw what he was holding. A camera.

He was filming her fucking herself at his desk while replying to comments. He was filming her being a filthy, horny slut.

Charlotte switched from one finger to two, but it wasn't enough. She went for three and jammed them as hard into her cunt as she could.

Her orgasm exploded, a furious shockwave that pulled every muscle in her body tight. She gripped Mamba's desk with her free hand and rocked under the force of her orgasm, her hips bucking, her clenched ass raised up off the seat. A scream pulsed from her throat, an animal-istic yell that went beyond language. Anyone who heard her would know what she was going through, what was happening to her.

And they would be jealous if they didn't already know the secret of how to have amazing orgasms like this for themselves.

When she came down enough to regain a sense of the world around her, Mamba was still filming. She could see him, though she lacked the strength to turn her head.

After another minute or so, Mamba lowered the camera and seemingly turned it off. He approached and stood by her.

Though once his presence filled her with dread and fear, she was comforted to have him near. Almost conversationally, she murmured, "I got your chair wet."

"That's fine, Cuntflaps. I'd make you lick it clean if it weren't for your amazing performance."

"Performance?"

Mamba leaned over her and jostled the computer mouse. Apparently, she had been cumming for so long that the screen had shut off. He moved the cursor over to the comment box she had filled with nonsense words. "Did you think I couldn't tell?"

She flushed, a little embarrassed. "You knew that I knew you were in the room?"

"Cuntflaps, I always know. I know your every thought, your every move."

"Does my screen show up in the video? Will anyone be able to tell?"

"You don't have to worry about that. This is for my private collection." Mamba chuckled darkly.

Charlotte looked up at him, though she kept her eyes demurely averted. "I'm so honored that I'm deserving of being in your private collection."

He had gone from wanting to ruin her to enjoying the sight of her. Thanks to him, of course, for recognizing her potential and forcing her to act upon it.

Mamba didn't waste too much more time with niceties. She appreciated that about him, that he was so truly his own self at all times. "Get out of my chair and go sit on the couch. I'll bring you your script. We still have a video to film."

Chapter Twenty-One

Open your mouth

ANOTHER DAY, ANOTHER VIDEO.

Even while Charlotte had that thought, she had a feeling this day wasn't going to be like the others before it. And that was because she had a plan. Well, a burgeoning hint of a plan.

A suggestion.

A request, really.

Mamba let her in and took her to his studio, as per usual. He handed her a script with his usual neutral expression, clearly expecting more of the same for the day. He must have thought that she had expended all her adventurousness the day prior. She was going to prove him wrong, she hoped. Either that or she would be playing right into his expectations, as per usual. She really didn't mind. It was nice to have a man who knew enough about her that he didn't have to be goaded into believing her ideas were his. He took charge.

He had always taken charge.

"Take a few minutes to look over your script," he told her.

Charlotte accepted the script. She didn't look at it. "Mamba?"

He paused while in the middle of turning away from her, eyebrows slightly arched in displeasure. "What do you want?"

Her stomach twisted, a combination of nervousness and excitement. "May I make a suggestion for a video to do today instead?"

He scowled at her, black eyes as sharp as steel. "You think you, a worthless cunt, are capable of handling your own video ideas so soon?"

She swallowed hard, ashamed of herself. Her pussy tingled to be dominated by him, his indomitable personality. "No, sir. Never mind. I'm sorry."

He sighed at her. "As you're already wasting our time, you may as well get on with it. What do you want? What's this idea of yours?"

"I want to keep being a source of education for my followers and subscribers," she blurted out, afraid that at any moment he would shut her down. "But I can't teach if I don't learn. I was wondering if you could... teach me... something?"

He ran his eyes over her naked, glistening body. She had once again gotten naked right in the parking lot in front of her apartment and had played with herself the entire drive. Thanks to the occasional bit of rough traffic, she'd sometimes had to put both hands back on the wheel. That meant her pussy-fucking hand had to get involved, smearing her juices on the steering wheel, and dripping them on her thighs and stomach. It had been such a fun accidental discovery that she had begun to do it on purpose, rubbing her juices on her stomach and breasts until she was covered in them almost all the way up to her neck. She looked, and smelled, like such a slut.

"What?" he asked, in his bored hiss.

"Teach me how to suck a cock so I can tell the girls. Please teach me how. Put your cock in my mouth and tell me what to do."

Mamba shook his head at her and for one heart-wrenching, disappointing moment, she thought that meant he was denying her. "Are you such a useless bitch you can't figure out what to do when a cock is in your mouth?"

"Yes," she agreed. "I'm a useless dumb bitch. I want to be a better slut for you."

"At least you know your place now," he growled. He dropped one hand to his pants, undid the button and pulled the zipper down.

Her disappointment dissolved into a fizzle of excitement as she realized what he was doing. Though she knew little about the act itself, she did have some idea of where she should be in relation to him. She dropped to her knees in front of him and waited, staring eagerly at his crotch.

Mamba reached in and pulled out his cock. He was half-erect, though stiffening all the while. "Hold my cock," he commanded, and let himself loose. His member arched against his thigh, a pulsating length of rigid flesh.

Charlotte reached for him, trembling like a person might reach out to try and touch a wild animal. Her fingers grazed his cock. His skin was surprisingly soft, almost delicate in texture, like the soft skin high up on her inner thigh, but stretched over the substantial and hardening length of manhood. She curled her fingers around him, letting him rest on her palm. She started to explore him with her hand.

Mamba grabbed the back of her head in his hand, digging his nails into her scalp. "This isn't a handjob," he snapped. "We aren't dating. I don't care if you get familiar with me or not. You're here to learn how to fuck."

She froze, startled, her hand unmoving in an attempt to keep him from getting angrier with her.

"Put my cock in your mouth, bitch."

I should only do what he says, what he wants. I risked enough by suggesting the idea to him. I don't want him to think that I'm trying to act out.

Charlotte leaned over him and opened her mouth. She felt the heat radiating from him as he slid into her mouth and closed her lips around him. His skin was so hot and he tasted salty in a very striking way that she hadn't been prepared for.

"Deeper, Cuntflaps."

She did as he bade, sliding forward on her knees so she could get more of him into her mouth. The texture of him on her tongue was indescribable. She could feel everything. The fragile softness of his skin, the expanses of hard flesh rippled with veins.

"Suck on me," Mamba commanded her. "You know how to suck, don't you?"

Was it really so easy as that?

Charlotte sucked.

Mamba swatted the side of her head. "Softer. Are you a fucking vacuum cleaner?"

Tears sprang to her eyes from the hard smack. Humiliated, she sucked gentler.

"Use your tongue. Lick me."

Charlotte kept sucking for a few more seconds, wanting to get familiar with the action. Mamba's hands shifting on her hair warned her to hurry up and get in gear. She hastened to do what he wanted and flicked out her tongue, trailing it over his erection.

"Do it more. Harder. Like you fucking mean it. Lick my cock."

I need to learn faster.

Charlotte put more effort into it, giving his cock long and fast licks. She tried to vary what she was doing, not just sliding her tongue over him but flicking him with it, curling her tongue around him, lapping at his swollen red tip. He was fully erect by that point, so either she was doing something right or he was getting off on yelling at her. Either way, he was hard, and she was happy about that. She was there to serve him, no matter what form that service happened to take.

"Use your teeth," Mamba demanded now. "Carefully. If you fucking bite me, I'll smack you so hard you forget your mother's name."

Her teeth?

She could never have imagined.

Charlotte licked her way back down his shaft and then, as carefully as she could, scraped his cock with her teeth.

Mamba let out an explosive groan that startled her, made her jerk away from him, fearing she had hurt him after all.

He grabbed her head and yanked her back, guiding her mouth back to his throbbing erection. "Good slut. Now move more. Fuck me with your mouth. Don't just sit there and make me do all the work."

She froze. Move more? She had no idea what he meant by that. What part of her was she meant to move?

She couldn't ask, not with his cock in her mouth.

Mamba growled with impatience and yanked on her hair. She yelped and moved with him to get the pain to stop, but then he shoved her head back, so hard she saw stars. Before she could recover, he pulled her forward again and then shoved her back once more. Another furious pull, followed by a quick push, forcing her head to make a sort of bobbing motion. Her loose mouth glided over his cock, up and down the entire time.

It suddenly clicked for her, what he wanted, what he meant by telling her to move.

Charlotte started to move her head up and down, following the rhythm he had shown her. Mamba loosened his grip on her head and she kept moving, working her mouth over his cock. His hips started to buck, following her motions.

Put it all together now, Charlotte told herself.

While she moved her head, she ran her tongue over his length, feeling him start to throb and quiver in her mouth. Her breath rasping in her throat, she added some sucking in, pulling him deeper into her mouth and letting him slide quickly back out. Soon she was almost pouncing her mouth on him, his tip striking at the back of her throat. The pressure wasn't bad or painful. She almost liked it.

But what mattered most was that he clearly liked it, as he bucked and ground in her mouth. She tasted the salt of his arousal and redoubled her efforts, ignoring the strain in her bowed back and the pain in her knees in favor of doing the best she could.

Mamba suddenly grunted. His fingers knotted in her hair.

Charlotte sucked as hard as she could and brought her mouth all the way up his shaft. She worked the tip of his cock with her tongue, curling her tongue around him and fucking him with it.

Mamba grunted again and sucked in his breath, as he always did right when he came.

It occurred to Charlotte, in that split second, that she didn't quite know what to do at this point.

No time to ask, or even to move away.

His semen jetted into her mouth, filling her with the taste of salt. It hit the back of her throat. Reflexively, she swallowed, feeling it burn all the way down her throat. More of his cum flooded onto her tongue and she swallowed again, and then he was going limp, wilting as the seconds passed.

Charlotte kept holding onto him, kept holding his cock in her hand. She didn't want to let go before she was allowed to. Something else might come next that she didn't yet know of.

Mamba pushed her off him. "Enough."

Charlotte withdrew, though she stayed on her knees. She felt like a woman coming out of a trance, slowly and in fragments rediscovering the world around her. She became aware that her pussy was pounding, a wash of her juices drenching her inner thighs.

Mamba tucked his cock back into his pants. His chest heaved a few times until he caught his breath. He straightened, lifting his head, and looked down at her without a hair out of place, looking as if he hadn't just been in the throes of orgasm less than a minute ago.

"Do you feel like you've learned enough?"

Charlotte nodded. "Yes, sir. Thank you."

"Go sit on the couch," he said, dismissing her with a careless wave of his hand. "I'll return to you with a script and a cucumber."

Cucumber?

He answered her without having heard her question. "To show the girls what to do. And then you can fuck yourself with it to finish the video. Try to save your cum for then, slut."

"Yes, sir."

Mamba left her, striding away without so much as a tremble in his step.

Charlotte watched him go and then got to her feet, smiling, with the taste of him still vivid on her tongue.

Chapter Twenty-Two

Role model

"I NEVER THOUGHT I would once again be reporting on this subject, but here we are."

Charlotte watched the television screen. The journalist, Windy Smothers, was the same one who had reported on her trial, that terrible event that seemed so terribly long ago. It might have happened to a different woman, so much time had passed since then.

"Charlotte Aria, the infamous content creator who angered so many people before with an outrageous video denouncing sex work, is once again making waves. This time, however, it's for a whole different reason."

An image showed upon the screen, of Charlotte as she used to be. Then, it was placed next to another, showing Charlotte the way she looked now, with her big fake breasts and platinum hair and more slender figure. Charlotte recognized the setting. It was near the grocery store she had gone to just a day ago. Someone had snapped a picture of her and presumably sold it to the news company, probably for a hefty price.

Windy smiled a little, lifting her eyebrows. "Perhaps I should say *famous* since Charlotte seems to have overcome whatever difficulties there were in her life to cause her to be so bitter and petty.

"As of three weeks ago, Charlotte's video channel returned. While all her old videos are still up on the platform, she has been making new content and the differences are astounding."

Two pictures again. First, of Charlotte in the past, sitting politely on her set bed, followed by an image of her lounging gloriously nude on the couch in Mamba's studio. Her hair flowed over the back of the couch, gleaming and healthy and fine, and her legs were spread so that her long cuntflaps were on display.

"Charlotte seems to have had a complete change of heart and has fully embraced sex as something a woman should be proud of. She now makes videos on how to enjoy sex, content which addresses subjects that young adults from backward, conservative homes might be curious about. But it's not only the sheltered teenagers who love her show. She is an accessible and passionate woman who is once again touching the hearts of many by being honest and forthright, discussing subjects with her audience that others might not so readily talk about with youths. Her subscriber count has tripled since her return. We have reports that she may have started a trend of sexual deviancy and degradation throughout the country. Time will tell what the consequences are of this, but I can tell you one thing." Windy smiled. "Our sons and daughters are going to be so much more relaxed with all the sex they'll be having."

Charlotte laughed, her heart full of pride. This woman had only half the story. Charlotte was the one who could see the direct influence she was having upon her growing audience. Yes, they were more relaxed, and they were happier, more confident. Every day, she received so many emails and private messages on all of her social media that Mamba was debating hiring someone–perhaps several someones–to take over for her.

Windy Smothers continued with her story. "I think we can all agree that we should be more like Charlotte. We should correct our faults and embrace our true selves. But that's all from me. This isn't a talk show and you don't want to hear my personal thoughts. We will, of course, continue to report on this story as updates come in. Now, let's go to Molly, live at the exotic bird cage at the zoo. Following a break-in earlier this morning, 70 parrots and..."

The TV turned off.

Charlotte looked over at Mamba.

He looked back at her.

They were in his house, in his second, smaller living room. He had invited her to come watch the news with him, having known ahead of time that they would be running a segment on her. Some source or other must have given him the intel. Either that, or he had been the one to set it up in the first place.

"I'm very proud of you, Charlotte," Mamba said. His voice held a rare warmth that she basked in eagerly. "You really have turned things around. I knew there was a slut inside you somewhere."

Charlotte gasped. "You called me Charlotte!"

"I did."

"But... who is Charlotte? I'm Cuntflaps. And I always will be."

Mamba gave her a very calculating look that went past her skin, penetrated her heart to a level underneath even what she thought she knew. He suddenly grinned and laughed and put his hand on her shoulder. "I should have done this to you years ago. I'm proud of you, Cuntflaps. Very few women could do what you did, coming back from the brink like that. Few would be so daring—or naïve—as to challenge me in the first place. A damn good job I've done on you."

She smiled, beaming at him, luxuriating in the praise she had been working so hard for.

Mamba led her out of his living room and to the studio, where she spent more and more time until it had begun to seem like a proper workplace. She could easily have logged onto her laptop at home and answered comments and emails from there; it just felt better to come to his studio and do it there, where he could watch her be the absolute slut he had worked so hard to turn her into.

Charlotte went over to her couch and lounged on it, absentmindedly playing with her pussy while he found her script for the day. He brought it over and held it out to her. She accepted it, her fingers wet with her juices, moistening the paper.

Embrace Sexual Freedom.

Charlotte glanced up at Mamba. "This script..."

He narrowed his eyes at her.

"Do you think it's time?"

"Did I ask for your opinion?"

She licked her lips. "No."

He nodded. "That's right. I didn't. Do your work and do it well. Earn your paycheck."

"My paycheck?" she repeated, eyes widening with her surprise. "I'll be getting paid today?"

"Only if you prove that you deserve it."

He walked away, leaving her there on the couch. Charlotte blinked a few times to get rid of the dollar signs in her vision, though it proved difficult to focus still. With how many views she was getting now, she could only imagine how many zeros would be on that check. Enough to restore some part of her life to its former glory, perhaps.

"I don't see you doing any reading," Mamba growled.

Charlotte ducked her head, hiding her face behind her script. She hardly needed to read what was printed there, since it was a story she had lived for herself. She waited a few minutes, moving her eyes, pretending to pay attention. At last, she said, "I'm ready to start filming."

"Already?" He snorted. "Do you think you're smart or something, to memorize it so easily?"

"I'm not smart," she murmured. "But I'm more in touch than I've ever been. I can do this."

Mamba was silent for a long moment. "Maybe you can," he conceded. "But if you disappoint me, you will regret it."

What will you do? Punish me? At this point, I'd like it.

She hid her smile behind a curtain of her platinum hair. She won either way.

Mamba told her to go when she was ready.

Feeling as if she had been born ready, Charlotte positioned herself just right, leaning back with her legs spread and her arms draped lazily over the back of the couch. She looked right at the main camera and spoke smoothly, calmly, and sensually, a huskier version of Mamba's hiss.

"Welcome back to Triple L. I'm your Host, Cuntflaps."

She paused, blinked slowly, giving her audience time to have their reaction. "That's right. Cuntflaps. My name is, of course, Charlotte, but I think of myself as Cuntflaps now. It's a very degrading name. And it's mine. And I am me."

"I think, after the past couple weeks, it's time to tell all of you what really happened in my life to make such a big change in me. I've been hinting at a lot of things, but I haven't been ready to tell the whole story until now."

Charlotte rubbed her hands on her thighs and smiled softly. "I grew up in a very old-fashioned, religious household where any boy I was vaguely interested in had to meet my parents. My skirts couldn't go above my knees and would preferably be down at my ankles. I was raised to believe in listening to the people older than me, supposedly wiser than me. When they spoke, I listened, and I never questioned them. So I grew up with my head full of absolute nonsense."

"Girls, we can't help the life we're born into. But that's not an excuse. I'm not my parents. I had plenty of chances in my life to take a look around and see how different the world is from the reality I was taught. I didn't. And that's why I grew up into a sex-hating, traditionalist woman with strict beliefs. I only took myself into account and ignored the rest of the world."

Charlotte shook her head at herself. "And that's just so wrong. I can't even put into words how stupid I was. The day that I made that video that got me into so much trouble, I went to a strip club called Lollipop. I saw people living their best lives, thriving on sexual freedom but I mistakenly perceived it as wrong and immoral. Stupidly, I made a commotion about it which got me into trouble. But it also got me into the sight of the very man who owns Lollipop. Mamba."

"Mamba has shown me the error of my ways. He's shown me things, aspects of myself I never had a chance to learn before. It's because of him that I have this hair color, these new breasts, this *lust* for life that I do now. He's given me the chance to transform from Charlotte into Cuntflaps. He's not just given me new hope. Through me, he's giving it to the rest of you."

Charlotte paused for breath.

The door to the studio opened.

Mamba whirled to his feet, staring at the open door and the intruder with an incredulous scowl on his face.

Charlotte remained on the couch, unable to comprehend the interruption. The only thing on her mind was wondering if she would need to redo this whole video. It seemed like such a shame to waste such an earnest performance.

Mamba marched to the door, shoulders tensed, like a viper about to strike. "What are you doing in here?" he demanded, spitting venom in his rage.

The intruder, a handsome man in his early 40s, backed up and smacked against the wall. He choked out, "You told me to come at this time," in a voice strangled with terror.

Mamba seethed. "*Tomorrow*. How can someone be so incompetent?"

Charlotte looked back and forth between the two men, wondering what was going on. The intruder held a camera, she realized. A photographer of some sort?

"I'm sorry," the intruder sputtered. "I can come back later. I..."

Charlotte knew the exact moment the man spotted her. His voice died out in a comical squeak and his eyes practically bugged out of his head. A huge bulge formed at the front of his pants, an erection that came on so quick it was almost like a magic trick.

This wasn't a new response. In the past few weeks, she had become more brazen about spending time outside. Men and women practically fell all over themselves for her at every turn. She had that sort of power over them.

An idea came to her on a whim, on a stray wind. Like a cat chasing a tumbling leaf, she pounced upon it.

Charlotte stood from her couch. "Mamba, sir."

"What is it you want, Cuntflaps?" he growled, not looking away from the man he was about to rip into. "I'm busy."

"He wants to have sex with me," she said.

Mamba's eyes flickered.

Charlotte pressed on. "I want to have sex with him."

"What?" the man squeaked. He jerked his head back, looking incredulous, but the skepticism was merely a mask for his pounding lust. His cock was practically tugging him to her like a magnet.

Mamba repeated the man's query in a lower, more dangerous tone of voice. "What?"

Charlotte approached, her heart fluttering in her breast. Angled cameras were capturing all of this, if Mamba decided to put it in the video. "This video is about how much I've changed and accepted who I am. What better way to prove it, to really show it, than to do what I want? And what I want is to have sex with this man."

"Why?" Mamba backed off and gave her a glare, one eyebrow raised. His lips curled into a smirk.

"Because he has a big cock," she said simply. "I want his cock."

"Is this for real?" the man exclaimed.

"It is." Charlotte smiled, very coquettish. "What do you say?"

The man looked back and forth between Mamba and Charlotte and then shook his head. "I never said no to a hookup in my life."

"Mamba?"

Wordless, Mamba left them standing there and crossed the room to the recording set-up.

The man shifted on his feet, nervous; however, Charlotte was non-plussed. She knew this was his way of giving permission.

Charlotte reached for the man's hand. "You're going to get to show off what you've got on camera."

No man could resist that. He grinned and grabbed onto her hand.

Charlotte smiled and pulled on his hand, leading him over to the couch. She pushed him down and sat beside him, still holding his hand. His fingers were very smooth and soft. She couldn't wait for them to dance over her body.

"Something unexpected just happened," Charlotte said, looking at the cameras while holding hands with her new friend. "I found someone I like, someone I want to have sex with. I've never met him before. I don't even know his name."

"Jeff," Jeff croaked.

"Jeff," she said, nodding. "I'm going to show all of you how much I really have changed, and how much you can change too if you follow my advice in these videos. Right here on camera, I am going to fuck this man I have never met, this man I will never see again. Maybe it will inspire some of you who are still on the fence... In any case, this is Triple L. And I will see you all in my future videos. I can't wait!"

With that done, she turned to face Jeff. She smiled at him and then leaned in to kiss him, pushing her lips on his with a fury. He gasped and grabbed her face, and then clutched her jaw, his nails digging into her skin.

"Slap me," Charlotte moaned into his mouth.

Jeff acted without hesitation, striking her across the face with the palm of his hand.

She cried out as a shock of pleasure flew straight to her pussy. "Fuck yes! Fuck me!"

Maybe in his daily life, Jeff was a polite guy. But there, on the studio couch, he turned into the raging sex machine all men want to be. He yanked his pants down far enough to get his cock out. While not as big as Mamba, he was thick and certainly big *enough*.

Charlotte wrapped her hand around his cock and lay back, spreading her legs to wrap them around him. She pulled him inside her, arching her back and lifting her hips.

Jeff thrust into her wet depths, filling her with his thick cock. He glided easily through her because of how soaked she was.

"Fuck me, fuck me," Charlotte chanted, bucking and grinding her hips against him.

Jeff lowered his head and bit at her sensitive nipple. He arched over her, fucking his cock towards the back of her pussy.

Charlotte cried out and held onto him with her legs around his waist, thrusting back at him.

Jeff gave a strangled yelp. He buried his face in her neck, biting and sucking at her soft throat. His hips jerked up and down. Charlotte moved with him, matching his pace, egging him on to go even faster. He jackhammered into her. Wet slapping sounds filled the studio.

Charlotte tossed her head, moaning, unable to hold still as the heat inside her built to uncontrollable levels. Jeff wasn't a particularly great lover, but she didn't care. He was using her, screwing her, reducing her to a sex doll, and she loved it.

Suddenly, Jeff pulled out of her. His semen hit her in the face, draped on her breasts.

"Slap my pussy!" Charlotte yelled, right on the edge of orgasm.

Jeff slapped her pussy, sending her juices flying all over the place. The glorious shock pushed her over the edge and she fell into an amazing orgasm.

"Thank you," Jeff rasped, straightening and pulling his pants up.

Charlotte smiled at him, still reclining on the couch, covered in juices and cum and with her hair all over the place. "My pleasure."

Jeff stood. He hesitated. "The picture..." He picked up his camera from where it had fallen onto the floor.

"Go ahead," Mamba growled, from across the room.

Charlotte stood up, too. "Where do you want me?"

Jeff's Adam's apple bobbed. "Just in front of the wall. And smile."

Charlotte positioned herself, hands folded behind her back to push her big tits forward. She smiled at the camera, knowing exactly how she looked and loving it, loving who she was.

Chapter Twenty-Three

Congratulations!

JEFF WALKED OUT OF the studio, moving unsteadily. He didn't shut the door behind himself.

Charlotte got up and shut the door herself. First, though, she peeked out into the hallway to see if she could see him. He had a nice ass for a guy. She was rewarded with a brief glimpse of his swaying rear before he turned out of sight.

"Come here, Cuntflaps," Mamba called.

Charlotte hurried to his side, eager to please as always. "Yes, sir?"

Mamba held out a thin piece of paper to her. "Amazing job. Amazing footage. You have absolutely earned this."

"My paycheck," she guessed and took the paper. Even though she had very much been looking forward to seeing how much money she had made, the amount no longer seemed so important. She would have been happy making YouTube videos for free; as long as she was able to explore her new passion, that was fine.

Mamba leaned back in his chair and gave her one of the best and truest smiles she had seen from him yet, showing genuine happiness. "You earned it," he repeated. "I look forward to seeing what you can do in the future, where we can go from here."

"Me, too." Charlotte tilted her head a little. She never used to do that before, but it felt like a natural gesture. Sluts were inquisitive. "May I ask you a question?"

"You have always been easy to figure out. That hasn't changed. You want to know what that was about."

She nodded.

Mamba glowered, no doubt at the memory of the unscheduled visit. "I told that damn photographer to come here and let himself into the studio *tomorrow*. And he didn't even get the time right. He was late. He's lucky you salvaged his visit, or he wouldn't have a job any longer."

"What did he want a picture of me for?" She wasn't used to people taking proper pictures of her. They normally snuck snapshots of her with their phones when they didn't think she was paying attention, though half of them were too dense to turn their sound down to avoid the very loud shutter click broadcasting their intentions.

"He's from Time Magazine." Mamba shook his head. "I'd expect better from such a prestigious publication. You are going to be given an award, Cuntflaps."

She blinked and did a doubletake, though his expression didn't change and he didn't take his words back. "Me? An award? What did I win?"

Mamba grinned at her, ebony eyes flashing. "Person of the year, for your contributions to Feminism and your phenomenal, inspiring story."

Tears sprang to her eyes. She rubbed her face, smoothing her hands over her hair. She had never imagined such a thing could happen to a person like her. It was simply overwhelming.

"You will be alerted soon, personally," Mamba told her. "I scheduled the photograph in advance. You will be summoned to give speeches at various locations. Oxford University has expressed interest in having you debate. My associates at the World Economic Forum have asked for you to attend the annual conference in Switzerland. Many important people want to meet you."

"I'm so honored," she gasped through her tears.

Mamba stood. He took a strand of her hair and gave it a near-affectionate tug. "You deserve it," he affirmed again. "I'm proud of you."

Charlotte looked up at him, the strict and dark man who had transformed her life for the better. "Can we celebrate?"

"And how would you like to do that?"

In answer, Charlotte got on her knees.

Laughing, Mamba unzipped his pants for her.

A year ago, she would never have believed she'd be alone in the home of a man she wasn't married to, or even dating, or even with whom she was friends, about to take his cock into her mouth. He was her boss, her manager, her guide into this wonderful and slutty world of which she had only scratched the surface.

She couldn't wait to see what else was in store for her, where she would go in this crazy life of hers.

But first, she had a blowjob to give.

Author's Note

Slutty whores win prizes in this world you live in, and modest women are laughed at.

Ridiculed and spat upon, too.

That's the world you live in, and you might as well get used to it.

Some women would rather sit alone with their thighs squeezed shut while all the rest of the girls go out and get their holes stuffed.

But not you, right?

You won't be a prude while all the girls go out there and get their hair pulled, their necks squeezed, their nipples pinched and twisted.

You won't lock yourself in your room while all the other girls are moaning and screaming and giggling and snorting with spit in their mouths, hands squeezing their asses with their cunts overflowing with hot cum.

Will you?

What kind of life would that be anyway? Looking out of your window while the world passes you by.

Might as well go out there and get some for yourself.

Right?

You'll feel so much better. So much more relaxed.

Besides, it's so much fun.

If you need inspiration for all that slutty fun, look no further than my book *Kelly Exposed*.

Kelly Exposed is a story about a sexually frustrated virgin who finds herself on a island of free sex. It's a cummng-of-age story, a tale of growth and transformation, and a celebration of freedom and pleasure.

It's just the kind of thing I'm talking about.

Give it a read, yeah?

books2read.com/KellyExposed

Love,
Viktor

Bonus chapter

FROM *KELLY EXPOSED* BY Viktor Redreich

"Women have a naturally submissive need for men."

I jerked my head up, staring around the auditorium. My gaze landed on the front stage and the man standing there. Even in my current state, he was so fine he took my breath away. His hair was black as night, while his skin gleamed gold like the sun. His broad shoulders and muscular frame gave him a raw beauty, like a wild and untamed animal. I was drawn to him, unable to look away despite my distant position.

This man must have been the Zion Carly referred to. Judging that the school bore his name, he must have been its head and founder.

I leaned forward to listen.

Zion placed his hands on the podium in front of him, big hands with long, strong fingers. "In this age, society has progressed so far that people forget the natural order of things. They have forgotten the proper place for women. That place is as a submissive to men. It is an innate, instinctual part of them. A woman's body is designed for sex, designed to receive a man's hard cock in not just her pussy but her ass and mouth as well. Do not let the words of others deceive you into believing otherwise. Accepting this fact is vital. All women are intended by nature's design to be sluts and do whatever men desire."

My jaw dropped lower and lower as he went on. He spoke in such a cultured and refined manner, every word delivered in a mesmerizing way. If not for the content of his speech, I would have already been applauding him.

None of the others in the audience found him as outrageous as I did. A few were even taking notes, scribbling furiously.

I'd do the same for my paper if I had anything with me.

"The clitoris has no purpose other than to allow a woman to feel pleasure," Zion said in his deep voice. "A woman's breasts are worshipped as a sign of fertility the world over. Her hips entice men to breed children with her. In fact, every part of a woman's body is designed to entice men. For what? As I have stated before, the answer is sex," he paused, sweeping his gaze across his captive audience; unfortunately, that also included me.

"Men, too, have roles that nature designed for them. By way of power above any of our comprehensions, man is made to be excited at the sight of women. This all means that women have a duty to be sexual and sensual creatures. By embracing a sexually liberated nature, a woman frees herself from the other restraints of society. Sluthood is freedom." He balled his hand into a fist and thumped it on the podium. "Let me repeat. Sluthood is freedom. By the end of your time here, you will know this freedom and embrace it with your mind, body, and soul. Welcome to my school."

Zion ended his speech, but with a powerful impact that made the other women in the audience screech and applaud. I was torn between giving in to peer pressure and refusing, which would make me stand out. Every part of me was torn, not just my mind. This weird man had moved me with his words and the conviction in which he spoke them. But what he said was wrong!

But was it wrong? Here on this island, everyone seemed to think it was right. I was so confused. My hands lifted of their own accord and patted together a few times in a flimsy façade of clapping.

Zion turned to leave the stage. Like he was a famous musician, the attendees closest to him rushed forward and blocked his exit. He remained aloof, as though his face was a mask, not even allowing a smile or a furrowed brow to wrinkle the smoothness of its surface.

Some of the other women in the audience appeared to remain in their chairs only because they'd swooned. They might think I was like them as if I could ever be counted amongst their number.

Never.

I would never allow myself to get caught up in what was happening here, no matter how handsome Zion was, and no matter how his speech made my heart pound. He had illustrated very clearly just now why the society here was the way it was.

It was an equality issue, and that issue stemmed from sex. Women were seen as inferior, meant only for the pleasure of others. That didn't fit with what Alora told me, but she wouldn't say it that way. As educated as she was, she was too deep in her own "sluthood" to see what that really meant.

But I saw it. And I would never, ever let it change me.

*

"Oh, Zion, I'm going to be the greatest student this school has ever seen! No, wait! The best *slut* the world has ever seen! Just you wait and see!"

I snapped my head up, my attention drawn again to the front of the stage by one of the girls blocking his exit. She positioned herself directly in front of him, her hands on her hips. She threw a dark look around at the other girls, daring them to defy her claim. The others returned her rotten eyes with their own, unperturbed.

I shrank back in my seat, my heart pounding. I hoped a fight wouldn't break out.

Zion stared calmly at the woman in front of him, still entirely unaffected by anything going on around him. When she felt his gaze, she turned and looked up at him with utter adoration. She was caught in his sensual web . . . The same web I might get stuck in if I wasn't careful. The man was so intricately beautiful, it was hard to think when looking at him.

"What's your name?" Zion asked the unabashed girl. His words were rich even when he wasn't projecting them into a powerful speech, a caress for the senses.

"Stephania," the woman answered, breathless. Her hands dropped from her hips. She sidled even closer to him like a puppy begging for attention, so docile compared to before.

"Well, Stephania, that is a very bold statement. You'll need to back that claim up. How will you do that?" The intonation of Zion's voice didn't change but it was a clear challenge.

I leaned forward, expecting what would happen at any other school when a professor called out a student. Stephania would recite a long list of why she could be the best slut, detailing incidents no one ever needed to know. Zion would nod his head and interject obligingly where appropriate before sending her back to her seat. No ground gained; no ground lost.

Instead of saying anything, Stephania dropped to her knees. She leaned to Zion and unzipped his pants, as naturally as she might do to a boyfriend in the privacy of her bedroom. She wore a dress so short that when she leaned forward, everything was on display. No panties, because of course, she wouldn't be wearing them.

I gasped aloud and put my hand over my mouth, unable to believe what I was seeing. Stephania reached into Zion's pants and brought out his member, and I had to gasp again because it was so much bigger than I thought any man's could be.

For the first time, I wasn't the only one shocked. The other girls in the audience were also gasping and exclaiming—except for an entirely different reason.

"Damn! That monster would tear my pussy apart!"

"Has that thing ever fit *inside* a pussy?"

"I could handle every inch!" someone claimed loudly.

Someone else murmured, "Lucky girl. I wish I thought of doing that."

I put one hand to the side of my head. I wanted to smack myself, pinch myself, anything to wake up from this absurd dream. Was this a prank? If I looked closely, would I be able to find hidden cameras recording my reactions?

Stephania ignored the chatter going on around her. Entirely absorbed in her actions, she proceeded to take Zion's member deep into her mouth. She clearly had tons of experience in such matters. She had no difficulty in working with him, despite how massive he was.

There was almost something erotic about the suddenness of it. My cheeks burned with shame to even think like that, but it was true. Stephania must really have been feeling something intense to give in to her basest desires like this in front of everyone.

"Impressive," Zion commented, ever unbothered even though one of his students was attacking him with her mouth. "But can you deepthroat me? That is the highest accomplishment of any cocksucker."

Stephania didn't pause for a second. She took up the challenge in an instant, tilting her head back and using her hands to guide his length deeper and deeper. She had no gag reflex, clearly.

But even she, a clear expert, couldn't take all that Zion had on offer. Several inches of his girth remained outside as she bobbed her head on him. Her hands stayed busy, performing tricks that would make a porn star want to ask for lessons.

It was so disgustingly impressive how much that other woman could take into her mouth and throat, and *still* have the mental power to pay attention to the rest of him.

Zion remained stoic above her; his face placid but his eyes burning with judgment.

Stephania upped her game, moving faster and faster.

Zion put his hand on her head and forced her off him. His gaze turned bored. I had to gasp again because he was unaffected by the blowjob he just received. He wasn't hard. Not at all. I was astonished to my core. Even I had been affected just by watching. How could he not be, having *felt* it?

"That was good," he declared. "But there is a lot of room for improvement. It seems you have yet to grasp the true meaning of the speech I gave. However, you have initiative. If you study hard, you will make a great slut indeed."

Stephania's emotions ran across her face for all to see, from joy to disappointment and back to joy again during her critique.

Zion retrieved a handkerchief from his back pocket and used it to wipe himself off. He folded the dainty square and put it back in his pocket, then zipped himself back into his hands. He turned back to the auditorium at large, the girl at his feet seemingly forgotten. "I regret to inform you all that I will not be staying for the rest of the day's activities. I assure you that you are in great hands with the professors and staff."

Then, he walked away without a single look back. The cluster of girls who had previously blocked his passage parted like a biblical sea to let him through.

What to read next

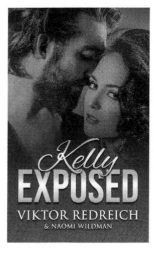

Read Now

books2read.com/KellyExposed

Also by Viktor Redreich

Books can be read in any order

Get your free copy of Dirty Secrets

Elyse said that she's been secretly letting a young man fuck her. He's her massage therapist and he was supposed to keep it professional but his hands kept wandering under the towel and touching her in places he *shouldn't* have been touching her.

One thing led to another and pretty soon he just peeled off his clothes. Fit body completely exposed to her, he climbed up on top of her, pushed her legs apart, and penetrated her.

Elyse isn't the only one having fun with younger men. Nicole is too.

In fact, Nicole told me that the college guy who lives next door to her has been watching her sunbathe in her bikini by the pool. At first, she was angry about him staring at her from his upstairs bedroom window. Soon though, she started to enjoy the attention.

Last I heard she even took her top off and rubbed lotion on her titties for him to watch.

Oh and you who else is behaving scandalously? Miranda.

Miranda's husband is a hunk and their sex life is great. She heard her husband bragging to one of his friends about how good and sexy Miranda is. How willing and eager she is. How she's basically up for anything.

Then out of nowhere Miranda's husband told her to suck his friend's dick.

Do you think that's going too far?

I think they're *all* going too far. Elyse, Nicole *and* Miranda.

What shocks me is how eager they were to tell me these things. How much detail they went into.

They really opened up to me. They literally told me *everything*.

Being a writer, I wrote it all down. Every dirty detail. All of Miranda's, Nicole's, and Elyse's secrets, plus the secrets of many other women just like them.

Just like *you*.

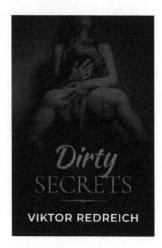

Get your free book now

Redreich.com/DirtySecrets/

Printed in Great Britain
by Amazon

50785290R00145